The Mitford Murders series

The Mitford Murders
The Mitford Affair
The Mitford Scandal
The Mitford Trial
The Mitford Vanishing

Jessica Fellowes is an author, journalist and public speaker. Her bestselling The Mitford Murders series has been nominated for awards in Britain, France, Germany and Italy, and sold into eighteen territories. Jessica is also the author of five official companion books to *Downton Abbey*, various of which hit the *New York Times* and *Sunday Times* bestseller lists. She has written short stories for *Vogue Italia* and *L'Uomo Vogue*, and made numerous appearances on radio, podcasts and television. She lives in Oxfordshire with her family.

The
Best
Friend

JESSICA
FELLOWES

SPHERE

SPHERE

First published in Great Britain in 2022 by Sphere

1 3 5 7 9 10 8 6 4 2

A CIP catalogue record for this book is available
from the British Library.

ISBN 978-0-7515-8395-3

Typeset in Horley by M Rules
Printed and bound in Great Britain by
Clays Ltd, Elcograf S.p.A.

Papers used by Sphere are from well-managed forests
and other responsible sources.

Sphere
An imprint of
Little, Brown Book Group
Carmelite House
50 Victoria Embankment
London
EC4Y 0DZ

An Hachette UK Company
www.hachette.co.uk

www.littlebrown.co.uk

To the memory of my mother,
Georgina

Contents

Prologue   1

Age Six   3

Age Nine   7

Age Fourteen   11

Age Seventeen   17

Age Thirty-One   51

Age Forty-Two   65

Age Seventy-Seven   225

Age Seventy-Nine   287

Age Eighty-Two   297

Prologue

In her mother's studio, as the sun faded gently, Georgie rifled through the assortment of abandoned papers weighted down by a painted stone: old bills, postcards from long-forgotten friends, affectionate notes from her late stepfather. She stopped and read one or two old letters, put some things straight in the bin, others to the side to deal with later. But she was stilled when she reached the photograph. The paper was curling at the edges, its shine and stiffness long gone. There was a white border and the image itself was lightly bleached, perhaps at one point it was in a frame and too much sun got to it. The picture was of two women standing close together, smiling, and though she couldn't see it, Georgie thought she could tell from their proximity, the angle of their bodies, that they were holding hands. They were of almost the same height, one slimmer than the other with dark hair, the other fair. The dark-haired woman was a touch blurred at the edges, as if she was laughing, unable to stay still long enough for the shutter of the old-fashioned camera. There was no one else in the picture, though someone had to be there taking it.

There was no indication that the women were interested in the photographer, though they were looking directly into the lens. Whatever was making them smile, even laugh, was only known to them.

Georgie stared at it for some time until she realised who it was.

History is black and white, she thought, but the past is all colour.

Kate and Bella.

Bella and Kate.

Bella / Kate.

SIX

Bella. *Bella*.

Yes?

What are you doing?

Drawing.

What are you drawing?

A rainbow.

Bella?

Yes?

Are you my best friend?

Yes.

Am I your best friend?

Yes.

For ever and ever?

Yes, Katie. Ever and ever.

NINE

I will be the queen, and you can be the handsome prince.

No, Kate. I don't want to be a boy.

All right, then. You be my servant.

Yes, a norphan.

What's a norphan?

You know, somebody whose mummy and daddy has died.

That's An Orphan, not a 'norphan'. Silly.

Don't call me silly.

Are you an orphan, Bella?

No. My mummy is alive but she is very ill and special people have to look after her. My daddy went to heaven when I was in my mummy's tummy.

You never met him? You never even saw him?

No. Can we play the game now?

Yes, call me Queen Katherine.

All right, but I don't want to be Bella in the game. Call me Penny.

Penny?

Yes.

Penny, fetch me my crown – we are going to go and find me a handsome prince.

What about one for me too?

But you're a servant.

Yes, but I'm a norphan too. My dead mummy and daddy were a king and queen. I deserve a handsome prince too.

Penny, fetch me my crown – we are going to go and find *two* handsome princes.

OK.

I never heard a fairy tale with *two* handsome princes.

This is *our* fairy tale.

FOURTEEN

Bella. *Bella.*

Yes?

What are you doing?

Trying to read my book.

What book?

You won't know it. Miss Frome gave it to me from the library.

What's it about?

I don't know yet really. A girl and her horse, I think.

An animal story. They're always sad.

I suppose so. It's OK so far.

Bella, I think Mr Garfield has a crush on me.

Do you? Why?

Because yesterday, when I went to ask him a question about the test, he went pink in the face.

What did you do?

I didn't *do* anything. You sound like my father. I can't help it.

No, I meant, when he went pink, what did you do then?

Nothing. I left him there, rosy-cheeked and stammering.

You're awful, Kate. *Incorrigible*, Miss Frome would say.

You and Miss Frome are ever so cosy these days.

She's nice to me, that's all. You don't have to make it sound like I fancy her or something.

You said it, not me.

Oh, for . . . let me read my book.

Hey, Bella. I'm going to go and get an apple from the kitchen. Do you want one?

What?

I'm going to go and—

No, I heard it. I meant: you're going to go and get an apple from the kitchen?

Yes. So what?

You're going to *steal* an apple.

It's not really stealing, is it? It's the school. They'd probably give us an apple later anyway, I'm just having it a bit earlier.

Hmm.

Come with me.

I've got homework.

You can do that later. You're so clever, you probably don't even need to do it.

I do.

Go on, come with me. Please.

Fine. I'm coming but if anyone sees us, it was all your idea.

SEVENTEEN

1

∞

Did you bring any candles, Bella?

Yes, one. I don't have anything to put it in, though.

Here, use this bottle. It's almost empty. Did you bring anything to eat?

Uh, yes. Some cake, slices of buttered bread, cheese, two apples.

Anything to drink?

Water. Couldn't find anything else.

No wine?

Not unless you're Jesus and can transform it, no.

I'm not saintly enough. You might be, though.
Saint Bella.

I'm not saintly.

Only teasing. I brought cigarettes.

They'll smell it.

No, they won't. We can hang out of the window. It'll be fine. I do it all the time.

OK. Kate, I keep thinking about Peter. When I saw him last week, I thought he was going to hold my hand. We were standing really close together, under the tree, and his fingers sort of brushed mine. I don't think it was an accident, I think he did it on purpose.

What happened?

I think I was so sort of surprised by it that I took a step back and then I couldn't get that close to him again without it being too obvious. And then the conversation came to an end, so . . .

Is he going to the party tomorrow night?

Yes, and I think I'm going to wear my shirt that's almost see-through, with lots of tiny pink flowers on it. I think he likes a very feminine look.

Why do you think that?

The woman who lives across the road from him, she told me.

What? Why did she tell you?

I had a cup of tea with her, we were chatting.

What, an old woman?

Hardly. She's forty-two.

It's more than twice our age. Trust me, that's old.

Well, she knows what she's talking about. She's known Peter since he was a baby, and she was really sweet – we talked about him for ages. She knew his last girlfriend and said she was very plain and not terribly bright.

So he'll definitely go for you, then.

Oi!

How did you even meet her in the first place?

She's a friend of Miss Frome's.

Oh, Miss Frome was there too?

Yes.

Bella, why act like you have to keep it a secret from me? We tell each other everything, remember?

Yes.

That's a good idea about the pink shirt, then. You can have my black trousers if you like because they're too big for me now. They'll fit you perfectly.

OK. Thanks.

We can go to the party together. Ask your granny if you can stay with me afterwards.

OK.

My mother never knows what time I get in. The other night, I got in at three and thought I was for it but no one said anything. Turned out they hadn't got in yet, either.

That's quite funny.

I suppose it is.

I think I should talk to Peter for you.

What do you mean?

At the party, tomorrow night. I can talk to him. Tell him that I think the two of you would make a good couple.

No, I don't think that's a good idea.

Why not? You're not going to do anything about it. It's been going on for months. You can't keep mooning about all over the place. *Something* has to happen.

But supposing . . .

Supposing, what, Bella-moo?

Supposing he doesn't fancy me after all. At least this way I don't know. I can dream.

You can't dream for ever, you've got to know one way or another. And it's very likely that he does fancy you. He nearly held your hand last week, didn't he?

His fingers sort of brushed mine. I might have imagined it. He was swaying a little bit.

Drunk?

I don't think so, but he'd had a beer or two.

I'm going to have another ciggy. Want one?

No thanks. What would you say to him, though?

I'm not sure exactly. I could just ask him about who he likes, or what sort of girl he likes, and then suggest you . . .

Hmm. I don't know.

I'd be very subtle.

Like you were with Mr Garfield, you mean?

Shut up. He was the idiot in that scenario.

What scenario was that, then? I meant what you said the other day, when he went pink.

It's too stupid.

Tell me, Kate. What happened?

We were talking, I can't remember what about, something I'd got wrong in my homework, and he'd asked me to stay back after the lesson. Oh, I don't really want to get into it.

Tell me.

He put his hand in my shirt, and just sort of . . . held it.

What? Left his hand there?

Yes, it was weird. He carried on talking. He didn't even acknowledge what he was doing. He didn't move his hand or anything. I didn't know what to do, so I just carried on standing there, like an idiot.

Did you mind his hand being there?

I don't know. Sort of. I didn't like that he wasn't even saying anything about it.

Then what happened?

After, I don't know how long, a few minutes, he took his hand out, and then he gave me this long look and said: that's between us, Kate. And I just nodded, and then I left the classroom.

Have you seen him since?

It was last week, we've had a couple of lessons but I haven't talked to him by myself.

Do you think you will?

Depends. If I need something, I might. Don't look at me like that, Bella. He's not that bad. A coward more than anything else. I'm only cross that I didn't tell him to stop.

He's your teacher – how can you?

You always can. Now, shush. We were talking about Peter, not Mr Garfield. I think you need to say something. And I can help you to do it.

OK, then. Maybe you're right. I can't go on like this. It's better to know one way or the other. And maybe there is a chance that he does like me. We do talk quite a lot. Last time, he asked me what I was reading and he seemed genuinely interested in the answer. He wouldn't do that if he didn't fancy me, would he?

Probably not, no.

Boys don't ask questions unless they want to kiss you, do they?

They want to rip all your clothes off, no questions asked.

Kate!

Only teasing. That's a plan, then. We'll go to the party together, I'll talk to him, then you'll kiss each other in the corner for hours and hours—

Stop it.

And we'll sneak back to my house. Your granny will never know.

2

The party was at Elaine's. Her parents were there but upstairs, letting the young ones get on with it, they said. Meaning someone could sneak in a bottle of wine to pass around, or some cigarettes, but if anyone was sick or *disruptive* (the oldies' favourite word), Elaine's mum and dad would be there like genies out of a bottle. Quite quickly, the knowledge that their babble was floating up to two pairs of listening ears became oppressive and the party moved out into the garden. It was late but the sky was cloudless and though the moon was not especially bright, their eyes soon adjusted and they could see the landscape of each other's faces, the glow of the cigarette tips.

There was an old climbing frame at the bottom of the garden, and two rackety swings, installed when Elaine was a small girl. Everyone began to converge around the childish playthings, sitting on the grass or leaning up against the frame with its splintering wood. There was a certain self-consciousness about it at first: it wasn't all that long since they'd been playing on the swings. Bella hadn't said much to

Peter, other than a 'hello', which had made her lips tremble. She was wearing the pink shirt with the tiny flowers and Kate's black trousers, which fitted around the waist but were too short. She kept pulling them down at the sides, which made her worry it looked like she had a nervous twitch, so she took swigs from her drink instead, to do something with her hands. She wasn't used to it and the wine had gone to her head already, not helped by the puffs she'd taken from Kate's cigarettes. Neither of them ate anything before they left the house, distracted by the business of getting ready, and at the party there was no food at all. The boys were starting to grumble that they were hungry, which made the girls nervous they'd leave, so there was a concerted effort from the females to entertain their opposite sex.

Bella sat on the grass, talking to another girl from school. One of the shy boys sat close by, not saying anything, drinking steadily from a bottle of something with no label. Homemade, perhaps. Out of the corner of her eye, Bella could see Peter perched on a rung on the frame, bending his head down towards Kate, who sat on the grass before him. She wasn't cross-legged, but had her legs elegantly folded to the side, a skirt spread around her. Kate's profile was tipped up, her dark hair falling away from her face and hanging even longer down her back. She flipped it around her neck and onto her shoulder, laughing at something Peter had just said. Peter leaned towards Kate a little more.

Bella's heart started beating faster and when she took a deeper breath, she felt fear expand inside her like a parachute opening in the sky. Fear at what she knew she was watching and for the confrontation she would now have to have. She took another drink of the red wine and a drop of it spilt onto her shirt. The girl beside her was drunk, endlessly talking – she hadn't noticed that Bella was no longer listening. Bella stared harder at Peter, willing him to turn his head and look at her, raise a finger in acknowledgement, give her a small smile.

Something, just for her.

He didn't do it.

3

I saw what you were doing, I *saw* it.

What are you talking about? Bella, you've had too much to drink.

No, I—

Here, have a glass of water. I'm going to make us both a cup of tea.

I don't want a cup of tea. I want you to admit that you were flirting with Peter.

Of course I wasn't flirting with him. I was talking to him for you, like we agreed I would.

Yes, we agreed that you would talk to him *about me*.

And I did that.

But I could *see* something going on. I could *feel* it.

You imagined it. We talked about a lot of things . . .

Ha, I knew it.

What?

You were tossing your hair about, making him laugh.
I should have been doing those things with him. I
hardly talked to him at all and you know how much I
was looking forward to seeing him.

You should have just come over.

I couldn't. There was a wall around the two of
you, it wasn't exactly inviting. You didn't look over
at me once.

I shouldn't need to, Bella! I'm your best friend—

Huh.

I am, you know I am. I don't know what you're
thinking, except I think you're perhaps a bit drunk and
we should talk about this tomorrow.

Don't patronise me.

Oh, for goodness' sake. Let's go to bed now.

I'm not staying.

What else are you going to do? You can hardly go back
home now. It's the middle of the night.

I'll walk.

Four miles in the dark? No.

What are you? My keeper?

I've put sugar in your tea. Drink it, Bella.

I don't . . . Fine. Did he even say anything to
you about me?

Yes, yes he did. He likes you.

He likes me?

Well, you know, you're a friend, aren't you? I wasn't
going to ask him if he fancies you. I said I'd be subtle. I
asked him what kind of girl he likes.

What did he say?

I can't remember his exact words—

Oh, so he didn't say *me*.

Bella.

He didn't say 'long hair', for example? Blue eyes.

He said dark hair, funnily enough, but—

Dark hair. Like yours.

Not necessarily like mine. It's not helpful to talk
about that bit.

The bit you suggested would so skilfully and casually
lead to talking about how perfect I am for him, you
mean? Fuck off, Kate. You didn't mean to help me at
all. You want him for yourself, don't you?

No, I don't. I can't help it if we get on.

You get on, do you?

I see what you see in him, that's all. It doesn't mean I fancy him.

What do you mean, you see what I see in him?

He's a nice guy, that's all. I get it.

And he fancies you.

I'm not going to have this conversation with you. I think you should go to bed, Bella.

But you're smiling, aren't you? I can see it. You're just waiting for me to leave the room and then you're going to be smiling and practically hugging yourself with fucking glee.

No. I am not. Go to bed.

I'm sitting down here until it's light, and then I'm walking home.

Fine. Suit yourself. You're so silly, Bella. I was doing it all for you, you know.

4

∞

Kate

I'm only writing to you because you borrowed my copy of 'A Room of One's Own' and it doesn't belong to me, it belongs to Miss Frome and I promised I'd return it. I'd be grateful if you'd post it back. You know the address.

Bella

PS Elaine told me about what you did with Peter. You bitch.

PPS You better return the book.

5

Bella woke when the light started to show through the curtains, a pale square with thin stripes on the calico. Her grandmother, in the next room, cried out, but Bella knew she would not get out of bed for a few more hours. The cries were rarely words, though sometimes Bella could make out *no*, or *please*, the tone always distressed. Her grandmother would snatch sleep in between and it was better that she lay in bed for as long as possible, recovering from the restlessness of the small hours. Bella would take her a cup of tea before she left for school.

Feet on the floor, Bella fought the urge to get back between the covers herself, where it was warm and dark and silent. She had learned it was best to get into the kitchen quickly and put on the radio and the kettle, to lose herself in the babble of meaningless clatter of mug, teaspoon, steam, music. She wiped down the surfaces and took a packet of mince out of the freezer, for supper. The night before, as had become usual, Bella had snuck the clothes her grandmother had worn yesterday from the chair in her room and put them in the wash. They were dry now, along with some of her own things, ready to be folded and taken upstairs. Half a mug of tea down, she straightened the sitting-room out and emptied the vase – the leaves of the tulips were rotted to a milky mush. She made sure to put the vase back in the same spot: her grandmother would tap it five times before leaving the room and on coming back in.

Was this what illness looked like? Bella didn't know. Her grandmother had always had quirks. At what point did those tip into something worrying, something that meant a fatal disease? There was no one to ask and no one to understand. Everyone else lived with their mothers and fathers in houses that looked, to Bella's eye, clean and organised with their neutral, empty walls and co-ordinated cushions. (What could these people know of oddities, when they were so frightened of anything *different*?) In her grandmother's house, the shelves were crammed with leather-bound books, their spines cracked and faded. On any given surface there would be an assorted collection of mismatching items, too small and strange to be dusted: jokes from crackers, chipped figurines, doll's-house furniture, egg cups that held the stones from broken jewels, glinting in the shadows. There were paintings on the walls of cold landscapes and people, long dead. Not that Bella minded any of this. The furniture was wonky but comfortable, the rugs were patchy but thick, the house was always warm. She felt at home there, and it was the only one she could remember living in. But she knew other people found it weird. They'd make too many comments, say too much the next day at school. It was easier not to ask them over at all.

Kate's house wasn't like anyone else's, either, but for all the good reasons. It was large and clean but not excessively so. There were well-chosen, well-framed pictures hung on all the walls, and large blue-and-white vases of pussy willow standing in the hall. The fridge was full, the washing up was done, the drinks cabinet was impressive. Bella had met Kate's father twice, briefly, a grunted acknowledgement; all the other times she might have bumped into him, he had been away, or at work, or a combination of the two. Kate's mother was more frequently home yet absent in her demeanour, always just coming in from somewhere or about to go out. Always looking beautiful, a heavy fragrance of jasmine hovering in the air around her. Her hands, briefly laid on Bella's cheek as she kissed her hello, were soft and manicured: they were not the hands that kept house. Bella yearned to go there, to sink on the armchair in Kate's room with a huge mug of tea and a plate of biscuits. To know that supper would be ready but only after they had had a long, hot bath. That they would be left alone to talk together, to listen to music, to plan, to gossip, to—

No. Never again.

(She missed her so much, though.)

Bella stopped. She had homework to finish and she really ought to clean the bath today. Then she would take her grandmother a cup of tea, reassure her she would be back later, try to persuade her not to buy more mints from the shop. The day had begun and Bella reminded herself that tomorrow had every chance of being better.

6

Hello, hello? Kate? Are you there?

Yes, I'm here. Sorry, I dropped the telephone. Is that you, Bella?

Yes, it's me. I need to talk to you.

What is it? Are you OK? I know what you think of me but I still care—

I haven't rung to talk about that. It's my granny. She's—

What? What is it? Oh, Bella. Don't cry, just tell me.

She's ill, I think. I don't know what's wrong with her. She won't go anywhere. She hardly gets out of bed and even if she does she won't get dressed, she sits on the sofa all day.

Is she eating?

Barely. She sucks mints, endlessly, to tiny slivers and hides the slivers under her pillow. I found handfuls there this morning. She's got a toothache but won't go to the dentist, keeps drinking whisky instead, to numb the pain.

She needs to see a dentist.

I know! But she refuses. Even though she's so vague about everything, she's as stubborn as an ox if you try to make her do anything. She has a photograph of a toad that she cut out of a magazine; she keeps stroking it and looking at it. I tried to take it off her and she practically spat at me.

How horrible.

It was horrible, Kate. I don't know what to do; I don't know who to talk to about it. I had to call you, I had to talk to someone.

What about the doctor?

I tried that but they said she has to go and see them, and I can't make her get dressed, let alone leave the house.

Then tell them they have to come and see her.

They won't listen to me, I'm not even eighteen yet. She's still my legal guardian. Kate, I keep thinking – what if what happened to Mummy is happening to Granny? What if that means it's going to happen to me?

You don't know that; you don't know it's the same thing. Don't jump to any conclusions. You have to talk to a doctor first.

What can they do, though? I can't see any medicine they can give her. What if they take her away and put her in a hospital for lunatics, like they did with Mummy? I'll be completely on my own then, Kate.

You won't be on your own, you've got me.

I can't exactly move in with you.

Maybe you could. You could sleep on the floor in my room, like you always do. It would be great, we could talk all night, every night. Or we could run away together.

I don't want to run away. I want to finish school. I want my granny to be OK.

What about Miss Frome? Maybe she could help.

I don't know. I'll tell her, maybe. I don't want anyone telling me that I have to move out, that's all. I don't want to leave Granny. I don't want her locked away. But I can't keep living with her like this. It's too much.

You need a plan of action. If you talk to Miss Frome, or try again with the doctor, they'll help you. I'm sure they will. I'm really sorry Bella but I've got to go now.

Oh, right. Sorry, I didn't realise. I didn't mean to interrupt anything.

No, that's fine, of course it is. I'm so happy you called me. I've just got to go now. But you'll be at school tomorrow?

Yes, see you tomorrow. Thanks, Kate. Bye.

Bye. I'm so happy we're friends again.

7

In the dark, they lay together. It was too hot to have anything over them. The air itself seemed to coat them thickly, like the damp breath of a tired dog. The tops of Bella's thighs rubbed together and she could feel the sweat slick and pool beneath her. They wore cotton knickers and nothing else, removing their bras under the cover of the night. Kate had opened her bedroom window as far as it would go but there was no cooling breeze, only the distant sound of a fox barking. They had soaked two flannels in cold water – as cold as it would get from the tap, anyway – and lain them on their chests, but after a few minutes they were already becoming uncomfortably warm. Bella thirsted but hadn't the energy to refill her glass; she lay there trying to call up the sensation of melting ice cubes trickling down her throat.

They both faced the window, watching the faintest shifts in the navy outlines of the trees in the garden, as they talked in no particular order about no particular thing. Homework that was late and the unfairness of the marks; missing hair grips; Lou's green nail polish; the horrible smell of the loos in the café; had Mrs Leiter really had it off with Mr Tucker?

Also: Bella's granny was no better. As well as the vase, she had to touch a particular silver plate twelve times when she both entered and left the room it was in. She refused to go to the doctor and the doctor had taken a week to come to her. He said perhaps she was depressed and wrote a prescription for pills. Bella got them but her granny refused to take them.

That was one topic.

Kate was going to a nightclub every Thursday night with three other girls from school, and they had seen Miss Frome there. She was kissing another woman. Bella didn't believe it but Kate said, hand on heart, it's absolutely true and everyone saw it. Miss Frome didn't see them. It was a crowded room and, besides, she only had eyes for one person. And that person was definitely a woman, even though she had short hair and it could sometimes look as if she was a man but Kate was certain. She knew what she had seen. It was hilarious and they had goggled at them, and danced, their shoes sticking on the floor from the spilt cocktails. It was sort of revolting but the whole thing was too funny. Even on the night bus all the way home they were in fits, and they had stayed at Lorraine's because her mother never asked any questions or even seemed to care much what anyone did.

That was another topic.

Everyone was doing the grapefruit diet that week. You ate half a grapefruit before breakfast and it burned twice as many calories of anything you ate afterwards, so if you ate nothing you'd burn up literal fat. Kate drank black coffee with her grapefruit and smoked a cigarette on the way to school. Bella was thinking about taking it up properly and maybe she would if it made her thinner.

At one point they laughed helplessly until they couldn't speak, at the memory of how Kate had accidentally called Emma Dunt, 'Shunt', their private nickname for her, to her face.

They didn't talk about Peter. Or Mr Garfield, who had disappeared without trace. There had been some rumours about him but nobody ever came forward to say anything. Car-park gossip, Kate said, that's what my father calls it. It was enough to see him off, anyway.

Bella thought: maybe I don't need to be completely alone.

In the stillness.

Kate's fingers brushed Bella's. Bella couldn't tell if Kate had touched her skin or if she felt only the static between them. Bella shifted the smallest fraction but hardly knew if she was doing it away from her or towards her. She made the tiniest move closer to Kate, so small she could say she was moving because of pins and needles. If challenged, which she wasn't.

The fox had stopped barking a while ago. The navy outlines were fading. Bella closed her eyes and there were dots of light that stretched under her eyelids. If she kept them shut, she could pretend Kate wasn't really doing what she was doing.

Which was . . .

Tracing her fingers faintly – as if her hands were gossamer threads, haunting Bella rather than touching her – tracing them over Bella's fingers, and now the back of her hand.

Kate's breathing changed.

Bella was conscious now, eyes opening before closing tight again. Her skin a canvas, Kate's touch as light as a paintbrush.

She dared not move at all, neither away nor towards the sensation. Kate's hand came down again and Bella felt the soft warmth upon her stomach, which gently rose and fell, more deeply as Kate's fingers went tip, tip, slowly south.

Just a little.

Just enough.

8

I don't understand. Why would they do it *now*? So suddenly? And what about school? Where will you go? Why can't you stay behind? Why do you have to go too?

Bella.

It's so unfair. What about us? Don't they care?

I've tried everything, they won't listen. He has to take the job, so we've got to go. They won't let me stay behind – who would I stay with, anyway?

You could stay with me.

I can't, we know that. Your granny . . .

Maybe only for a short while, to buy some time, to work something out.

It's no good. They've found somewhere for me to finish school. I've got to go with them. They are my parents, after all.

You don't seem very upset.

I can't cry any more, that's all. I've had days of shouting and crying, and they won't budge. The decision has been made. It's final. Et cetera.

What will I do without you?

You'll be fine, don't be silly.

You always call me that. Don't call me that any more.

Sorry. I am sorry. I don't want it but I don't see what I can do. It doesn't have to be for ever. In less than a year I'll be eighteen and they can't tell me what to do then.

They'll give it a good go.

Maybe. But we can keep in touch, we can write.

You never write letters, you've said it yourself.

I will now, for you. Of course I will.

You'll find another best friend.

How could I? There's no one else in the world that I've known since I was six. That I like.

Really?

Really.

I feel as if you're being all grown up and I'm a child.

We almost are grown up, Bella.

Well, I don't feel it. I don't think I want it.

Want what?

To be a grown up. A part of me wants to stay in school, always.

Ugh. I definitely don't want that.

Well, all right. Maybe not always at school. But to stay young, to stay like this.

I want freedom. I want to go and live where I want, with whom I want. I want to go out, to wear red lipstick and have red nails.

Without anyone telling us what we can do and when we have to get in.

Exactly that! Did you hear Elaine went to—

Yes, I did. I couldn't believe it. Did her parents find out?

I don't know. Probably not or we'd have heard about the punishment. She told Mercy, who told me.

I didn't know you talked to Mercy.

Only a bit. We sat next to each other in French, when you were doing Spanish.

I see. Is she nice?

Who?

Mercy.

Oh, yes. She's quite funny. She wears unexpected things, I like that. She's not predictable.

No. Kate, do you think we should do things differently?

Like what?

I was thinking about maybe cutting my hair shorter.

Hold it up a bit . . . like that, if you tuck it under, you can sort of see . . . Yes, I like that. I think.

I'm not sure. Maybe. When are you leaving?

At the end of term.

That's only two weeks away.

I know.

I won't see you again, somehow I know it.

You don't know it. I'm not leaving the planet, just going to another part of the country.

A very distant part of the country.

Yes, and I'm the one who has to go and leave everything behind. You might think about that, Bella. I won't know anyone there. I bet Old Fish Head sends a terrible letter ahead and they think they're getting the naughtiest girl in school – I'll get a hard time as soon as I arrive.

I know you're right. I'm sorry. But you're beautiful and everyone loves you. You'll be Miss Popular in seconds.

You won't be there.

No. I won't be there.

But we will write.

Yes, of course. We will write.

And then we'll meet.

And then we'll meet.

It's not the end.

No, it's the beginning. Of something else. A new chapter.

A whole new book, perhaps!

THIRTY-ONE

1

All over town, the bill posters went up, seemingly overnight. On her walk from the train station to work, Bella counted four of them. When she went to the café at lunch with a colleague, she saw two more. They were striking not only for the sheer number of them but for the aggressive lettering in red, white and black, mimicking an outraged headline on the front page of a newspaper. Bella noticed them – how could she not? – but it was only on the second day that she realised the posters were advertising a new play starring Kate Maddox.

Kate.

After Kate moved away, fourteen years ago, Bella waited for the letter that would tell her the new forwarding address. The exit, made in haste, had taken Kate and her family first to temporary lodgings, from where they were going to look for their new house. Kate had assured Bella that she would write as soon as she knew where she was to let her know the new address, would tell her what the new school was like, would make plans for them to meet in the long holidays. But the letter never came. Not from one week to the next, nor in the months that followed.

Bella had no idea what town Kate was in, let alone what school, or street. There was no one to ask, no means of discovery. As the weeks had passed, she was at first afraid of what had happened to Kate, but that was soon followed by fury. Bella felt cornered, as if Kate were forcing her to beg for the friendship

It wasn't long before anger gave way to grief. Another loss to bear.

In the year she remained at the school, Bella felt Kate's absence as a constant, piercing pain. Her mind would forget that Kate had abandoned her and then each time she remembered anew, the shame of rejection would flood her senses. Without Kate to talk to, the dam was broken and Bella's dialogue rushed inwards and was sharply critical. It made perfect sense that Kate wanted no more to do with her: she was not pretty enough, not clever enough, not *enough*. Needing distraction, she took a job as a part-time nanny with a family, cutting lessons to collect the children from school, take them home, feed them, bathe them, put them to bed. Then she would go home and do the same for her grandmother. There were no more than pockets of time left to herself, which suited her perfectly. Bella would overhear the other girls at school talking about boys and parties, the electricity of their youthful excitement almost visibly sparking off them, while Bella had been switched off. She could not think beyond the next hour at a time, moving steadily from one necessary task to the next.

On the rare occasion Bella tried to talk to someone about Kate, she was shut down. It was as if mentioning her name might summon the dark gods that could bring discord to all. Once, with Miss Frome, Bella mentioned the mystery of her vanished friend and Miss Frome shook her head, putting her finger to her lips. When Bella asked why they must be silent, she received only the same mute response. It became an obsession for a while – what was this secret that everyone, including those she had thought were her friends, was keeping from her? It gnawed at her with an empty, incessant sensation. The same that kept her from eating, even while she chewed constantly on pencils and ground her teeth at night.

There was one tiny clue. Bella walked past two giggling girls in the school corridor, who clamped their hands over their mouths and widened their eyes as she walked past. She knew it was deliberate. They wanted her to know that they knew something she didn't know. She asked them – *what?* – and they shook their heads before they burst out laughing in gasps of mild hysteria, gulping in air, clutching each other's arms.

What?

She put her hands in her pockets, physically restraining herself from slapping them. One, the smaller of the two, started to talk.

Mr Garfield's coming back—

Her friend snatched her shoulder, hissed at her to stop.

No. Mum said—

But she shut herself up, looked at Bella, standing there, stricken, mute. They ran off, the soft soles of their regulation shoes slapping on the floor, the white lights overhead somehow brightening at their exit.

If Mr Garfield returned, Bella didn't know. She left the school early, before the final exams, only a few weeks after her grandmother was admitted to hospital. It was two long bus rides to see her but Bella did it every two days for six months, and then once a week for a year. Then, rarely. She was ashamed at her inability to make the journey and the shame turned her love for her grandmother into another silent secret. When she died, Bella realised even as she mourned that she had been granted the freedom to do what she wanted.

Bella lived now in another part of the country, where she knew no one of her old life. Any collision of worlds, her past and her present, had been kept so carefully apart, that it was hard to believe she wasn't hallucinating Kate's name on the poster. The sunlight had already begun to fade the red lettering. At half-past seven, every night except Sundays, and twice on Thursdays and Saturdays, Bella knew where she could find Kate. After the final curtain, it would be no more than a matter of knocking at the stage door, and asking to see Miss Maddox. Bella didn't even consider the possibility of Kate refusing to admit her. She knew, in spite of everything, that Kate would want to meet again.

2

Two nights later, Bella sat in the auditorium of the theatre. It was almost full. She had taken a seat by the aisle, in case she wanted to leave quickly. A middle-aged couple sat beside her, the woman smelling strongly of cough drops, her hands nervously clutching a crumpled handkerchief. She looked at Bella apologetically just as the house lights went down. There was the gentle rustle through the audience as people put down their programmes and adjusted their feet, the whispers of hastily finished remarks, the last-chance sweets unwrapped and popped into mouths, the sitting back with pleasant expectation for the next two hours.

The production was a good one. A simple but effective set – a newspaper office, in the main – and costumes that looked as if they would be worn by the characters rather than mannequins. The writing was sharp and funny, set at a pace rarely seen on the stage. Kate didn't appear until the second act but she was a pivotal moment in the plot. Bella studied her closely, enjoying the fact that she could watch Kate without Kate knowing she was being observed by her. She looked beautiful, or rather, more than that – powerful. She played a young, promising journalist, brought in to bring hard-bitten editors to their knees with her ability to get scoops worthy of the front page. Her talent made the editors jealous, and one in particular sought to weaken her with various threats and manipulative jibes. There was one moment, shortly before the intermission, which happened on the far stage left, so close to Bella she could see the faint line where Kate's wig was glued. The editor, played by a man who had been a big star in his youth, grabbed Kate's wrist in the middle of their argument and Bella thought she saw genuine terror pass quickly over Kate's face. She almost reached out of her seat to save her.

After the play ended, and the cast took three curtain calls, Bella slowly gathered her bag and coat, running over in her mind the reasons she had told herself earlier she would go straight home. She did not need Kate. Alone, she had built a life: she was painting, and doing well, almost well enough to leave her office work. She had met someone, and she was hopeful they would marry soon. There were a few girlfriends she would meet up with from time to time: they were pleasant company, demanding nothing from her. She would go home.

Only, in the street, watching the audience stream out of the theatre, hearing the lively hubbub of their chatter as they discussed what they'd thought of the play, she realised she couldn't walk away with them. Kate had already thrown her a rope and was pulling her back in.

3

Minutes later, Bella was following the stage door man along a line of corridors, painted dark red and sparsely lit by bare bulbs. Then, a line-up of dressing-room doors, open to release the smell of cheap champagne and the fevered talk of friends congratulating the actors. Too soon, the doorman was knocking on Kate's door, her name written on a piece of card that had been slipped into a small brass frame.

Who is it?

The doorman looked at Bella and she told him her name, too shy to say it herself. He repeated it, saying it twice in quick succession. There was silence and then the rattling of the handle before it was pulled wide open.

Bella?

Kate gave the doorman a nod and he scuttled off.

It really is you?

It's me.

Kate kissed her on both cheeks and gave a wide smile.

> Come and sit down, I've got some wine open. I wish
> it was champagne now you're here. This is such a
> surprise, I had no idea . . .

Bella walked in, feeling awkward with her coat hanging
bulkily over one arm, her bag held underneath. The temper-
ature in the dressing-room was stiflingly hot, and the room
itself was barely larger than a cupboard, dominated by a long
mirror with white bulbs all around it. Beneath was a narrow
shelf stacked with the usual actress's kit: face powder, lipsticks, several pots of cream, flowers, good luck cards, a full
glass of wine. A wig sat on a life-size head, blank of features.
Kate was prattling on, seated before the mirror, taking out
grips and removing the thin stocking-like cap, shaking out her
dark hair beneath. Her stage make-up was thick and garish in
close-up but Bella could see the girl she had known beneath.

> Just take those things off the chair and sit down. I'll
> find a glass for you.

Bella sat and took the glass of red wine Kate offered her. It was
too warm but she sipped it gratefully. There was the briefest
moment of silence as they sat opposite each other and then
they both spoke at the same time.

> How did you—

I know it's a surprise—

Kate stopped, put her hand up.

You go first.

I saw the posters.

Do you live here?

Not too far on the train but I work close by.

Goodness, how extraordinary. We're on tour, only here for a few nights, then off to godknowswhere. It's always a bit of a blur, I'm afraid.

Yes, I can imagine. It was a wonderful play . . .

Bella-moo. I'm so pleased you came to see me.

I wasn't sure whether you'd want to see me or not.

Why on earth not? *Of course* I'm thrilled.

You left, and I never heard from you again.

Kate waved her hands in front of her face and took a large gulp of wine.

That's all so long ago.

Bella nodded. She felt suddenly oppressed by the heat and the nearness of Kate.

Why didn't you write?

Oh, I don't know. I was young and selfish. I wasn't thinking properly. There was so much to do when we got there, looking for a new place and then getting settled into the school.

Yes.

Kate topped up their glasses. Her smile was bright, photo-ready.

Come on, tell me how you are. What are you doing? Do you work? Or are you married?

I work in an office, nothing interesting, it pays the bills. But I've been going to art school—

I don't remember you painting.

I didn't. I drew a little, for myself. I didn't have the confidence then but I think I do now.

Yes, I know what you mean by that—

There was a knock at the door and the costume assistant came in to take Kate's stage clothes away for cleaning. Bella waited quietly while Kate stripped off down to her underwear, not bothering to conceal herself, then put on a Chinese silk dressing-gown.

Where were we? Yes, tell me, are you married?

No. Not yet. But I think I will be soon.

Without thinking, Bella put her hand on her stomach, then removed it. It was very early days, she couldn't know for sure. It was just a feeling.

Well, I'm sure you have a treat in store. Don't ask me,
I'm an old married woman.

Kate slumped back in her chair and drained off her glass.
Bella saw that her skin beneath the powder was ashen. The
smile had disappeared, as suddenly as a switch.

I don't mean to put you off. Forgive me. You've come at
a funny time.

Sorry, I—

No, it's not for you to be sorry. I don't—

I had to see a doctor today. I thought I was pregnant.
And it turns out that I was, I am. No, stop—

Bella had been about to get out of her chair.

It's not viable, he said. I don't even know what that
means. Except that it means I'm not pregnant. Or
shortly about to be *not pregnant*. You know, the
ridiculous thing is that I didn't even think I wanted to
be but just in those brief moments, I thought I was and
I was terribly happy. Isn't that silly of me?

Kate started to cry. This time, Bella did get out of her chair.
She knelt beside Kate and put her hand on hers.

I'm so sorry, Kate. I wish I knew the right thing to say.

There's nothing to say. I hadn't even told—

Bella stood to look for tissues on Kate's dressing table but Kate wiped her face with her hands and gave a final sniff. She put her hand on Bella's arm, to stop her from doing anything.

Please. Let's forget about it. Are you free now? We could go out, get something to eat. There must be somewhere open.

Bella regarded her old friend. Her eyes red, the thick make-up now smeared, her hair falling flat. She looked small in the chair, her back to the wall of the tiny dressing room, with its cracked linoleum floor, the sound of exiting parties with the other actors echoing in the corridor. Bella tried to discern what she felt. Sadness, yes. But also: sangfroid? That Kate should not be untouched by misery. That she might know something of what Bella had felt.

No, I'm so sorry, I can't. I have to catch the last train home. Good luck with the rest of the tour, Kate. I hope it goes well. You were brilliant tonight.

Kate nodded. She understood. She breathed out a little shakily, poured out some more wine for herself.

Of course. It was lovely to see you, Bella. Perhaps we'll meet again, soon.

Perhaps.

They kissed, and Bella exited, leaving Kate behind.

FORTY-TWO

1

Bella thought it was her, but she couldn't be absolutely sure. The weather that day was *filthy*, as her great aunt used to say, as if the sky needed a good clean. The sunlight that struggled through the grey clouds was hazy, leaching the colour out of everything, and perhaps it was that which meant she couldn't be quite sure of the profile. Or was it more that there was something in the walk, and the angle of her back as she leaned down slightly to listen to the boy beside her? Her son? Most probably, about eight or nine years old. Something about her posture, the fact she was there with a child, made Bella think that there was a permanence about her in this part of town. Not passing through, on tour.

Bella pictured herself running up, touching Kate on the shoulder, seeing her spin around, smiling as she did so, a fixed upturn of the mouth only. The eyes would register a moment's confusion, then delight, when she realised it was her old friend.

But she didn't do it. She stayed where she was, her feet fixed on the pavement. Bella didn't want Kate in her life. Not here, not now.

Bella looked down at her left hand, the gold wedding ring on her fourth finger. It gleamed on the curve, showing up the tiny scratches it had gained since she first wore it. Her hands, of which she had once been proud, with their long fingers, showed a network of faint green veins under the pale skin. The knuckles looked red, as if sore; her fingernails were cut so short the fleshy tips were tender when pressed.

Not here to stay.

Not now.

2

Bella?

Kate.

My goodness. How long has it been?

Half a lifetime, I think. It's funny, I thought I saw you in the street, a week or so ago.

Did you? Why didn't you say hello?

I wasn't sure it was you. And I wasn't sure—

That you wanted to talk to me again? I can't say I blame you. I disappeared that first time, didn't I? I've thought about that. I'm not completely made out of stone, in spite of what everyone says.

Kate stopped a passing waiter, took a new drink off the tray and passed it to Bella before she took another for herself. Bella took the opportunity to study her, appraising her like a new subject in her studio. A slim form with a shape that was defined by well-cut clothes; hair still as dark and glossy as a stallion's, shorter and neater than when she was seventeen. Skin that was smooth, only just beginning to lose its elasticity around the jawline, the nose long and straight, the mouth generous.

Since you mention it, and I wasn't brave enough last time we met, I have to ask: why did you?

Disappear?

Yes.

Oh, I wish I knew. I think I was trying to fit in to the new place, and when I thought about you, it all seemed so heavy and sad. I think it was too much for me, everything that was happening with your granny. I didn't understand it, didn't know what to do. We were seventeen, we didn't know how to behave properly, did we?

I suppose not.

What happened to your granny in the end?

She died, twenty-one years ago. She went into a home and faded into death. My mother had died six months before.

I'm so sorry.

Yes. Well. It was pretty gruesome, that whole period. You vanishing into thin air was . . . bewildering, most of all. I couldn't write to you because there was no address. I tried writing to your old address to see if anything would get forwarded but . . . I suppose it might have been but there was no reply.

I'm not going to try and excuse myself.

You were seventeen?

OK, I know how pathetic that sounds. I'm not looking for forgiveness. Only – I am here now. I'd love for us to meet up again. I remembered you lived in this part of the world. I hoped you'd still be here.

You live here now?

Yes, we moved a month or so ago. Charlie is starting at the school.

Charlie is your boy? I think I might have seen him with you.

Bella wondered if what had passed between them before would be mentioned, or if it was to be kept packed away, like outgrown clothes.

Yes, he's eight. What about you? Have you got any children? I can see you're married.

Bella's hand went to her ring. She gave it half a twist.

Yes, to David. Eleven years. And we have Georgie, she's almost ten.

So we both have onlys?

Yes, I suppose we do. There was a time I wanted another, curiosity I suppose, as much as anything. I'd like to know what boys are made of. But it's just the three of us and I'm so used to it, I prefer it.

Yes, I agree. Just the one is easy. You hardly need to change your life at all. I put off having one for years because of work, can you believe? But the work dried up and then . . .

No, it seemed. They wouldn't be discussing what went before.

Who is your husband? I don't think you said.

Alex. We've been married nineteen years. I was practically a child bride. But we met and it was one of those whirlwind things. It was nine months from soup to nuts.

What?

From our first meeting to the wedding, I mean. It was nine months. It's one of my uncle's expressions. I don't even know what it means. Does one finish several courses with nuts?

That's funny. What does he do?

Alex? He works, a money thing. It's not uninteresting but the explanation of it is. And I suppose I've spent too long with people who never ask about his work.

How is that?

Because actors aren't interested in people who wear suits to work.

What about you? Are you interested?

I try to be, for Alex's sake. I miss my actor pals, though.

How come?

Oh, when one's not in a play, somehow one's out of the loop. I had a few good parts in my twenties, rather fewer in my thirties, and as good as none now I'm at the age I dare not say out loud. I can't hide it from you though, can I?

No, you can't.

There's quite a lot I can't hide from you.

What are you hiding from everyone else?

Bella knew she was being disingenuous. She still held the key to Kate's cupboard of secrets.

Oh, Bella. What are we all hiding? Our lumps and bumps, our fears, our grey hairs.

You don't have any grey hairs.

That's what I pay someone a lot of money every six weeks to make you believe. I've had grey hairs since I was thirty-four.

Do you pay anyone to hide your fears?

73

What, lie on a couch and tell a stranger with a notebook all my deepest, darkest fantasies? No thanks.

I don't quite mean that but I take the point.

Why, do you see someone?

I did, for a bit. A few years after my mother and granny died. I was trying to leave a job I was unhappy in, and they didn't want me to go, or said not to leave until I had found something else, and I started getting panic attacks. I thought I had better see someone but after the first appointment I was offered a job, and when the second appointment came around I was feeling fine again, and we both agreed I didn't need to go back.

What was the job?

Nothing particularly. Not relevant to what I do now, anyway.

What do you do now?

I'm a painter. Portraits.

Yes, of course you are. I think I saw a review for an exhibition of yours a few years ago. I was pleased to see that art school had been the right move for you.

Yes, it was, surprisingly so. I mean, it's rather to my amazement that that's how I earn my living, and it's not a bad one. David's income can be unreliable.

Why?

Bella finished her drink. She looked around vaguely, to see if there was somewhere to put down her glass, but also to stall her answer to the question. The room they were in was large and generic, with blank walls and a stark lack of any attempt to prettify the situation. It was filled now with women, mostly of a similar age to her and Kate. The only man in sight was elderly, collecting glasses slowly and carrying a tray that looked as if it was too heavy for him even when there was nothing on it. Bella watched him sympathetically for a moment.

Bella? You went away there for a moment.

Sorry.

Why is David's income unreliable?

Oh, well. *He* is unreliable.

I don't like the sound of that.

I don't mean to be disloyal. He's very loving, it's not that. He's not got a wandering eye, or roving hands. He's a bit lost, I think. He's never quite found what he wants to do.

What has he tried?

Quite a lot. Painting, as in decorating. Public relations. Something in the City for a bit. Journalist. He thought about training as a teacher.

I see.

The problem is that he doesn't like working for anyone else, but if he works for himself then that involves a certain level of administration that bores him.

But he does meet his responsibilities? To you and your daughter?

Yes, he does. Then again, I do quite well, with my paintings. There isn't the pressure on him, financially I mean. Sometimes I find it quite useful – he'll be the one at home, looking after Georgie, when I'm in the studio.

How radical.

It isn't, not really. It's just that we prefer that Georgie is looked after by one of us, rather than a stranger.

They're not strangers for very long, the people who look after your child.

No, but you know what I mean.

I do, Bella. I always did know what you meant.

Even when no one else did.

Especially when no one else did.

3

Bella held a lunch for Kate, inviting four women she knew and liked who lived close by. Each of them had at least one child that went to Georgie's school. Years ago, when grieving Kate's sudden absence, Bella decided she would no longer risk the hurt that could be inflicted by a single 'best friend'. Like swearing off lovers, it was simpler to be celibate on that front. Friends would be carefully and slowly cultivated over the years, chosen for their complimentary qualities to her and each other. That was the plan. As it turned out, she became friends with people simply because they lived nearby.

But these women were all of a type that she felt would please Kate: they took care of their appearance, had wit or brains, sometimes both. She knew she could rely on there being no awkward silences and, importantly, they would easily show their affection and loyalty to Bella. She had not known these neighbours more than five years but they had shared some significant moments. Their children had begun school, Theresa's child had been frighteningly ill for a few months, there had been a cancer scare for Jenny, a divorce for Charlotte. She knew they were not her tribe; for a long time she missed the closeness she had had with Kate but told herself such intimacy was only possible at a certain stage of one's life. She knew the mothers' sense of humour was not quite the same as hers but that wasn't to say she didn't laugh with them. They shared no history, knew nothing of Bella as she was at school or as she was when she emerged into the world, rudderless without her grandmother, her parents dead. They hadn't even known her as a disorientated bride in the early years of her marriage, or the long days when she thought she would crawl out of her skull with the boredom of looking after a two-year-old child alone. When she and David moved to this house, she embraced the opportunity to change things. Having told her husband that she had no interest in making friends with 'other mothers' – women she dismissed as having no conversation beyond their children and domestic duties – it became apparent she needed to change tack. Her daughter needed friends, for a start. And there was no denying that Bella needed support outside of her marriage, even one forged in the shallows of proximity. And once she paddled in, joining the conversation at the school gates and on the coffee mornings, she came to see that her prejudices had been mistaken. The women were friendly and kind towards her, their conversation moving swiftly on from their domestic cares. Soon, she felt guilty about the assumptions she'd made before.

She looked forward to showing off this new life of hers. Bella would cook a delicious lunch – simple yet sophisticated – and set out her prettiest plates and napkins, a white cloth on the table. There would be elegance in a relaxed atmosphere, with possibly even the faintest note of subversiveness when she brought out the chilled champagne and a box of cigarettes before one o'clock. Why not, she would say, with a smile.

Kate was the first to arrive, which threw Bella off, as if the first person in the audience had come onto the stage by mistake. They kissed hello and complimented each other on their hair, their shoes, their style. Kate admired Bella's cushions, flowers, paintings on the wall, some of which were her own work. They were studiously polite, each eager to show willing to make this work, to atone for past hurts and to praise for present accomplishments. They both knew where the other had come from, and what it had taken to be there now. What they didn't know, in the stark daylight, was how to recover the trust they had had before. Bella wasn't even yet sure she wanted that intimacy again, wasn't certain how good Kate had been for her back then. But there was something palpably exciting about being beside someone she knew so well. Even after two decades, there were gestures that were familiar, phrases she recognised. When Bella made Kate laugh she felt as if she'd been awarded a gold star by a teacher.

Tell me who the others are.

They're all mothers at Georgie's school but I do think you'll like them. Charlotte's quite acerbic but she has a heart of gold. Theresa is half-Italian—

Glamorous, then.

Yes, she is, and Jenny is great fun – first on the dance floor.

A good collection. It's sweet of you to introduce me to them, though all I really want is to talk to you, you know.

I promise you we will, but it's good to know some others nearby – we help each other out quite a bit with the children. Jenny has a boy about Charlie's age.

Yes, Charlie could do with some friends. I'm not sure he's settling in very well to the new place.

Give him time, it's only been a few weeks. How is Alex finding it?

Oh, fine. He's at work for most of the time, I don't think he thinks about it very much. So long as I'm getting on with decorating the place and not moaning too much.

Do you need any recommendations? Theresa's house is beautiful, I'm sure she'll know a good handyman or two.

And so on. They talked in this light, superficial way, with Bella half longing to pull Kate into the cupboard under the stairs, like when they were young, to talk in the half-darkness with a huge bar of sticky chocolate.

In the event, Jenny turned out to be in the mood for an extravagant afternoon and they followed her lead without much persuasion. The first bottle of champagne was polished off fast, and then two more bottles of wine were guzzled during the lunch, which was a hit. Kate claimed she was such a bad cook that she had once – while admittedly very drunk – served herself and a guest dog food sandwiches, and neither of them noticed. The three friends were in turn awed and delighted by Kate's stage career, and she entertained them with hair-raising stories about the casting couch and actors who were so vile she would deliberately eat bulbs of garlic before a kissing scene. Bella swelled with pride.

When four o'clock arrived, it took them by surprise, everyone hurriedly pulling their coats on and checking their eye make-up, giggling that it was practically illegal to go to the school in such a state. Kate asked Jenny for her telephone number. Bella was just fetching the recipe for the pudding for Theresa when she overheard the exchange and shocked herself with the jealousy she felt. She told herself not to be so absurd: hadn't she invited everyone so that Kate could have these new friends, to help her settle in?

If she was truthful, that wasn't it at all. She'd invited them to show off. To have Kate's glamour rub off onto her, to make Jenny, Theresa and Charlotte jealous. To make them believe that her past was filled with friends like Kate, women who might appear at any moment and show up their diminutive lives. She'd wanted Kate to be green-eyed with envy that, in spite of the fact she had dropped Bella like a used handkerchief, Bella was a highly prized friend these days: connected, central, fashionable and fun.

The alcohol and cigarettes had left her mouth dry, and she could feel a headache beginning to press at the base of her neck.

The person she had most wanted to fool was herself.

And she had failed.

4

Hello?

It's Bella. Is it a good time to talk?

Yes, perfect. I've got nothing on for at least an hour. How are you? I meant to say at the lunch how extraordinary and lovely it was to bump into you at that odd little drinks thing. And now it's led to this, us talking on the telephone again.

I know. I thought the look on Mrs Richter's face was very funny when she realised we knew each other.

Who is she?

The local busybody. That's quite mean of me but she's not someone to tell your secrets to, put it that way. She'll already be dining out on us having known each other as schoolgirls.

It's not that interesting, is it?

It is around here. How are you settling in?

Fine, I think. We're getting our bearings. Alex's drive into work doesn't seem too awful. Charlie likes the school, or he's not hating it at least. I'm not generally keen on getting to know the neighbours, apart from your nice friends of course, but there's a friendly wave here and there already.

That's good to hear.

My stepson, Randall, will be coming down to stay this weekend.

I didn't know you had a stepson.

No. He doesn't live with us.

Do you get on?

I'm not the reason his parents separated, which helps. He's good to Charlie. But he's not working, which maddens Alex.

I know the feeling. David has chucked his latest job, or it's chucked him. I'm not quite sure which but it amounts to the same thing, doesn't it?

Not really, Bella. The difference between someone being fired and someone resigning is reasonably large.

I know that. Only, it means he's without a job either way.

Do you mind? You said before that you like him being at home.

I like him being around to look after Georgie when I'm working.

Ah, I see. Not quite the same thing.

No.

Bella paused. The light in her studio was starting to fade and she liked it most then. There was something about dusk that felt like the quietest and most private time of the day.

What does he do when he's not working?

He cooks, using every saucepan in the kitchen but the results are adventurous. He'll track down exotic ingredients for days—

Days?

Sometimes. He decided once that he wanted to make the perfect curry, I can't remember what type it was. Indian, something that reminded him of his childhood. He found a tiny shop in the back streets of God knows where. That's what he said when he came home after three days.

Are you sure he doesn't have a wandering eye, Bella?

Yes, I am sure. I know it sounds as if I shouldn't be but he's incapable of lying. He can't even play Cluedo. I can see it in his face the second he tries to hide something from me.

Hmm.

Please, Kate. I'd love for you to meet him, you'll understand then. Why so quick to suspicion?

Because it doesn't take much for a man to look elsewhere. But mainly because you don't seem happy.

I am happy. As happy as anyone has a right to expect to be. Besides, no marriage is perfect, is it?

Is that a veiled question?

Sorry. I don't mean to pry.

I'm teasing. No, of course no marriage is perfect. I'm so glad you rang. I wanted to ask you and David over on Friday evening. About seven. We're having people over for drinks. Nothing riotous.

That doesn't sound like the Kate I knew.

Ha ha. Alex is going to be there, that generally keeps things on the right side of sensible. Or wrong side, depending on your point of view. If I get bored I might liven things up.

How have you only been here a short while and already you're throwing parties?

It's not a proper party, just drinks. We knew some people before we moved. That's partly why we're here. And then, Charlie's school and that's how it is, you meet parents, don't you?

Mmm.

I'd love to meet David – please bring him. No need to dress up.

That means: find your prettiest dress.

I'll be wearing a pretty dress but that's because that's what I like to do. It doesn't mean you have to do it too. Wear whatever you want.

Perhaps I'll know one or two other people there.

I'm sure you will. They all live locally. I'll ask Jenny, too.

Can I bring anything?

No. Alex will have all of that in hand, he likes doing that sort of thing. You and I can concentrate on getting ready.

Yes. Remember when we used to spend hours together before a party? Long discussions about what we were going to wear and how we were going to do our hair.

More fun than the party itself, usually.

Yes, it was. The anticipation of what was going to come before the crushing disappointment when the boy paid no attention to you. That happened to me, not so much to you.

It happened to me.

I can't think of any boy you wanted to look at you who didn't. What about Peter?

Honestly, Bella. Are you going to bring that up?

I can't help it, Kate. It still stings a bit.

It's been a quarter of a century!

Yes, but it made me feel so small.

I didn't mean for that, you know I didn't.

Do I?

You should know; you should have known then.

I was a young girl, who had liked him for such a long time, and talked to you about it. I couldn't believe you would kiss him.

Barely, it was the tiniest kiss. He leaned in and I forgot myself for a moment, no more than that. Bella, I can hardly even remember it.

I know, I know. I'm not going to go on about it, I promise. But I couldn't not mention it at all.

Yes. Now you have. Come on, then. Friday, seven o'clock. You know where we are. See you then?

See you then. I'm looking forward to meeting Alex.

And I am looking forward to meeting Unreliable David.

Don't call him that at the party, please.

I won't. See you on Friday, Bella. Goodbye.

5

Over the next few days, whenever the telephone rang, it triggered an increase in Bella's heart rate. She hoped it was Kate at the other end, with all the feverish excitement one felt for a new lover. (Would it be them and what mood would they be in? If there was an arrangement in place, the excitement would change to fear: were they telephoning to cancel?) Bella assessed the clothes in her wardrobe. Everything seemed shabby, destined not to impress. Old favourites were too well worn. She couldn't buy anything new: it would be too obviously fashionable, too try-hard. She couldn't even seem to decide which colour looked best against her skin. Black could be chic or mawkish, depending upon the mood. Bright palettes too naïve. Pastels were wrong for the season. A long dress too formal, a short one too sexy – and was she too old for sexy? Forty-two. It made her sigh each time she thought it.

Her hair could do with a cut. Was it absurd to book herself an appointment? Bella wasn't extravagant when it came to spending money on herself, not like some she knew. But she didn't stint, either. There were creams on her dressing table that cost more than dinner for two in a good restaurant. She knew the importance of keeping one's figure as one got older. She declined puddings during the week and walked everywhere. Kate was probably much stricter, her collarbone definition demonstrated that. Bella would eat as little as possible in the three days before the party. Then, perhaps if she did her make-up carefully and wore her one pair of very expensive shoes, she might get away with a simple dress, an 'old thing'. There would be people there she knew, after all. She wouldn't want them commenting on a radical departure when it came to her look on the evening.

And there was the fact that she was an old friend of Kate's to bestow glamour in her direction. At the very least, Bella could rely upon Kate to stir up the neighbourhood. She left a smattering of star dust in her trail wherever she went thanks to her work as an actress, even without her having had too many big parts recently. Mere association was enough – her past proximity to leads such as Hazel Dennis and Mark Warwick had the power to blind people with the dazzle ten years on. (Bella wanted to ask very much what it was like to kiss Mark Warwick, and whether they were real kisses or a clever juxtaposition of the lips and chin.) Besides that, Kate had the 'actress glow', a look underscored by years of carefully practised eyebrow shaping and a knowledge of which dresses flattered best, thanks to advice from costume designers.

Bella pulled back her jawline again, tried not to sigh.

She was caught in this friendship again, whether she liked it or not. Not only a lack of choice, but of clarity, too. Given how they had parted before, was Kate on her side, or toying with her, like a kitten with a mouse? Would they play together or would the kitten ultimately attack the mouse when it had had enough of the game? Which instincts were closest to the surface?

At the party, Bella would find out.

6

In the middle of the party was a swimming pool. One came across it without warning – not even a smell of chlorine or humidity in the air. On arrival, Bella had walked through the garden with David, and she supposed she was distracted somewhat by the sight of the people before she noticed anything else. She saw only those that were close up, as if she was walking along a wall, like a child tracing brickwork with their fingertips.

The guests appeared as a dense collection of dark, shimmering fabrics, with little skin revealed. There were fast-moving red mouths, with white teeth. Ghostly strands of hair brushed her face as she went by. The scents were exotic – lilies, tuberose and jasmine – mingled with cigarette smoke and whispers, occasional laughter crackling in the atmosphere. It was, she imagined, like walking in the Amazon rainforest at night.

The pool was large and angular, the water moving, rippling the underwater lights. No one was in it. A solitary inflatable swan floated on the top. She wanted to jump right in, feel her feet touch the solid bottom of the blue-tiled floor, and then push back up and up, holding her breath as if the very air inside her could make her rise faster.

Someone touched Bella on the arm. David had left her side, gone to talk to a man he knew.

Bella looked at the person, who was rather smaller than her, and elegantly dressed.

Forgive me. I'm a friend of Kate's. She asked me
to find you.

Bella nodded and followed him, walking away from the watery temptation.

Kate was standing in a circle of six or seven people, all of whom were turned towards her, listening. She held a glass of clear liquid, from which she frequently sipped. There was a faint smudge of her lipstick on the rim. Her eyes were large, darkened by tricks with kohl, lively and expressive. In any room she would be the most beautiful woman there; Bella knew this, and Kate did, too.

Bella, darling. Come here, you've met Mighty, I'm so
pleased. He's my favourite man. This is—

There followed a list of names, instantly forgotten.

Bella wondered in how many strides she could reach the pool, if she could jump in wearing all her clothes, and whether the water would be warm or shockingly cold.

Kate took her hand and held it.

You must hear this, too. It's a true story, it happened to my aunt's friend, Lucie. She was staying somewhere enormous, a monstrosity of a place. There seemed to be fifty bedrooms, some of which connected to the one next door, some had a small dressing room attached with a single bed made up in it. Lucie had accepted the invitation to the house party, though she was nervous about it. However, her mother helpfully reminded her that she was twenty-eight years old and unmarried, and not in a position to refuse. So she had gone.

Kate let go of Bella's hand, the better to gesture with.

On her third night there, Lucie was sitting at her dressing table getting ready for dinner, when a good-looking man with blonde hair walked out of the door that she knew led to a room with a single bed in it. He came out of that little room, walked behind her – she saw his reflection in the mirror – not looking at her, apparently rather harassed but not saying anything, and went straight out through the door to the hall. It gave her a fright. She was sure she had checked the adjoining room and had thought no one was staying there. She looked for him amongst the party but didn't find him. He had been wearing distinctive round wire-framed spectacles but there was no one of that description, not amongst the guests nor the servants. She asked around but was met only with puzzled looks and she feared people thinking she was a spinster on the edge of going dotty, so didn't pursue it much further.

Cut to three years later, Lucie walks into a restaurant and she sees this man – blonde, specs – sitting at the bar. She couldn't help herself, she walked straight up and asked him if he had ever been a guest at the Mullins's party. No, he said, he'd never heard the name.

I know you can guess the rest: they fell madly in love, quite quickly, and were married. About a year or so after their wedding, Lucie received another invitation from the Mullinses. She went, with her husband, and asked to be put in the same room as before. The housekeeper had an efficient system, she'd made a note of where Lucie had been and there they were installed. Lucie told her beloved new husband: this is how it was, it was you, I swear it. We must re-enact it.

Her husband loved her but he was becoming rather irritated by this story. He tried to put her off and reminded her that they were due downstairs for dinner shortly. Lucie insisted, it wouldn't take long. She would sit by the dressing table, he would come in from the door of the small adjoining room, walk behind her and out into the hall. He agreed, he would do it, just the once.

He did it.

She never saw him again.

Kate drained the last few drops of her drink before she turned to look at Bella.

She never saw her husband again.

94

7

It had been so long since she had been to a proper party that Bella had forgotten how they worked. Kate had obviously underplayed the event, or perhaps in her world even a drinks party was a more extravagant affair. Bella didn't know how many people were there, as she kept stumbling across more of them every time she walked to another part of the garden or through the house. She knew some from seeing them locally, and stopped occasionally for a brief conversation or merely waved hello. She spent a lot of time making it look as if she was on her way somewhere, so as not to have to make strained conversation with someone she'd only met once or twice before. Strained for her, anyway. The rhythms of speech and cadence, the questions and answers, seemed beyond her this evening. In her nervousness she'd quickly drunk too much.

A couple of times she saw David, standing before another man, his drink held close, his head tilted forward, listening closely, warding off any other interlopers – even his wife. She left him alone. Kate was, inevitably, caught up with her guests, her arms always aloft, always mid-embrace, her glass threatening to spill. She introduced Bella to one or two others and then immediately drifted away, leaving them to make awkward chat about how they knew Kate, where they lived. It was easier to duck out of Kate's eyeline, to find the drinks.

There were waiting staff, young and good-looking, and two bars set up, one inside, one in the garden. A large white tablecloth hiding boxes of champagne beneath, silver buckets of ice on top, constantly replenished glasses.

Music came out of the house and into the garden through the French windows. Bella heard a song she liked, and swayed gently in the shadows. Two of the waiting staff were kissing in the trees. She thought she saw Kate being pulled along by the arm, by a man she didn't recognise. Even in that glimpse, she could see that something tethered them together, a shared look of subterfuge. Bella dismissed the thought. She was probably wrong and it was nothing to do with her. She went inside, needing a long drink of cold water. To find David. She knew, if she was good, she'd go home now, pay attention to the tap-tap that told her she'd had enough.

But she didn't want to be good.

8

When the night was cooler, and the older or more sensible contingents amongst the guests had left, the rest of them came inside. Kate drew the heavy curtains, and the lamps were low. There was a row of candles burning on the mantelpiece, softly lighting the old, speckled mirror that hung above. The music was loud enough to hear without trying, quiet enough for a lover's whispers to be heard if leaning in close.

Bella hadn't seen her husband for some time. Kate moved between the people, lightly touching an elbow here, a waist there. Her glass was never empty. Bella watched Kate. She herself was standing, alone, in the corner of the L-shaped room. There was a vast mirror hanging on the wall at the end of the shorter arm of the room, giving the illusion of an even larger party happening. Bella caught herself, had half a second where she didn't fully realise she was watching her own figure shift. Her movements appeared timorous, yet she wasn't afraid, merely less flamboyant than those around her. Their bodies were pressing closer together as their hips swayed more widely.

Kate came up to her, her hand in a closed fist. She parted it slightly, held it up to Bella.

Take this.

Bella didn't resist. How could she? She swallowed the small blue pill.

Come with me.

Her fingertips touched Kate's then they broke apart as they weaved through the dancers into the very centre of the room. Kate looked at Bella, smiled, then put her hand on her waist and drew her in a little closer.

Bella smiled back. Kept her eyes on Kate and they moved together. They laughed as they spun each other around and tossed their hair. Then a man came up, and put his arm around Kate, winked at Bella.

Alex is drunk.

Kate mouthed the words and Bella caught them. Someone turned the volume of the music up. They had met earlier, briefly, formally. She gave a wave as he twirled Kate before him, feeling rather spare now. Wondered where David could be – had he noticed her absence at his side? If he had, he'd think nothing of it. Alex was tall, broad shouldered, with prominent eyebrows in a face that looked soft, like a cinnamon bun.

As she stood there, something shifted in the atmosphere, the beat of the music slowing, going deeper. The lights seemed lower, the flames of the candles grew longer. The bodies pressed closer and Bella saw a man come towards her. He had an intent in his eyes that she had not seen for a long while directed at her body, her face. She felt her own beauty come to the surface of her skin, creating its own heat. The rhythm in the music thrummed at the very core of her, sending waves, a rise and fall of inner sensations that reverberated through her limbs. As he neared, he kept looking at her until she was certain their heartbeats were matching in speed. Lightly, his hands lay on her back and, almost without knowing it, certainly without deciding it, she pressed the length of herself against the hot air that lay densely between them. She wanted to close her eyes but could not. She knew she might fall if she didn't keep watching. He filled her vision entirely but she could only see parts of him. His skin was young, smooth; his white teeth showed, his eyes were ice water. She thought: my heart can fill, then break, then fill again.

She felt her mouth tremble and yearned to submit to his desires. Or were they her desires? There was a gentle persistence in her mind that told her to remember David – but he was not there; he seemed so far away. She felt herself on the edge of a cliff and all she wanted to do was step off, not to jump but to fly.

Who are you?

He shook his head. He was a secret. Of course, he was shadows and caves. She saw him look around and tried to follow his eyes but only he was in focus. He took her hand and she felt the dryness of his fingers, the cool of his touch, and it soothed her. She concentrated very hard on feeling the ground beneath her feet but it was too difficult. It seemed to lurch and slope like the deck of a ship. Nausea rose up fast and she jerked his hand, signalled her urgent need.

Quickly, he pulled her out and she kept one hand in his, the other on her mouth, and they ran out of the room, down a dark corridor, up a flight of stairs. Was there another set of stairs? Or another passage? She couldn't remember, focused only on her mouth and her feet, hardly using her eyes except to check that one foot followed another. There was the opening of a door, and then she felt the cool of tiles beneath her knees as she bent over and expelled herself.

In the dark, there was a line of light. Was she supposed to follow it? Where did it lead towards? And then, it disappeared. In the black, she retched again.

Bella leaned forwards further, her arms wrapped around her head, felt the roiling in her stomach move its way through her, could almost picture it as a pulsing liquid, a witch's brew. The light fell across her again, and she tried to turn to see behind her. Her neck was too stiff, she couldn't manage the effort for long. Thought she saw someone hesitating in the doorway. She couldn't make sense of the shapes. An arm, a tilt of the head, soft breathing. But man or woman?

Kate?

The white line gone again, the door clicked. Bella lay down.

When she next opened her eyes she was fully upon the hard floor. Sweat beaded her forehead. She shivered; her legs were exposed. She felt her hips pulled up and back. She looked for what seemed a very long time at a dark corner where dust had gathered and she concentrated hard on the faded colour on the tiles, imagining herself as a tiny dot that flew into the furthest, darkest reaches until the pain subsided.

Later, she woke again, alone, and cold. She washed herself and threw the flannel into the bin, then went downstairs to find her husband. She hoped he was still there. She had no idea how long they had been apart: minutes, hours or years.

9

Bella told no one.

10

Georgie got into the bed, cool and quiet beside her mother. Her small hand lay on Bella's shoulder, shaking it gently. Beneath her nightclothes, Bella's skin was red, sore to touch in the places where she had scrubbed hot water and soap until the pain lifted to the surface.

Mummy?

Bella willed her eyes to stay shut. Colours vibrated unpleasantly and nausea kicked in her stomach. She opened them, saw the sunlight leaking behind the closed curtains. The air she breathed was sour and the sheets damp.

Mummy? Will you get up now?

No, darling, I'm not feeling well. Please, go back downstairs.

When will you come down?

I don't know.

Bella tried again to block everything out. Failed again.

Her mind was both full and empty. There was no whole memory, only scraps of things. And no knowledge of how she got home. Was David with her?

Is Daddy here?

Yes. He gave me eggs for lunch.

Bella's eyes sprang open at that; she concentrated on breathing, trying to make the nausea go away. There was no hope of getting out of the bed, let alone the room.

Georgie, I love you.

I love you, Mummy.

But I need to sleep now.

OK.

She felt her daughter slide out of the bed and pad softly across the floor, the door clicking behind her. Bella stayed in the same position, her eyes watching until the light faded into darkness. She wanted only to feel pain, but nothing came.

11

∝∘

When Bella got up, the house was completely still. Georgie was at school. David was – where? Not there. Again.

She suppressed the feeling of gratitude, of relief. She knew what she had to do: get dressed, brush her hair, go into the studio, pick up a brush and paint. Keep going. At four o'clock she would collect Georgie and tell her they had things to do together: make a cake, and eat it, possibly before it was baked. They could lick their fingers, it would remind her how to laugh. If Bella couldn't be alone, the next best thing was to be with her daughter. That was good. David's absence was perhaps even thoughtful of him.

She didn't want him gone, not altogether. But just for now, yes.

Yes.

Please, stay away. But not for too long.

12

Kate? Kate? Are you there?

Yes, darling, I'm here. What is it? You sound terrible. I haven't heard from you in—

It's David. He's gone.

What do you mean? Gone where?

I don't know where. He went – he went a few days ago.

How many days?

Four, on Tuesday.

And he didn't tell you he was going?

No, of course he didn't. There's no note, no message.

The first thing to remember is that if anything really awful had happened, you would know.

How would I know?

The police would be at the door. Presumably, they're not?

No. Perhaps you're right, it means he's alive at least. But how could he just go? I didn't think he'd do it again.

Again?

It's not the first time.

I gathered that. Come on, Bella. Tell me. I can't help you unless you talk to me.

It was when we were quite new together, I think it had been six months—

When things were getting serious.

Yes, I suppose so. All I knew was that we were madly in love. We spent almost every night together when, without warning, there were no telephone calls, no notes, no arrangements. I nearly went out of my mind. It was only then I realised that I knew nothing about him: I didn't even know where he lived.

You'd never been to his house?

Flat. No. I know it seems ridiculous now but at the time it was easily explained: his work was near my place, so we'd meet there to go on somewhere. It was more convenient. And he said he had a lodger, so he didn't want me staying there.

I can see how you would go along with that.

Exactly. I couldn't ask his work where he was because we'd met there, and there was a strict rule about work relationships.

You could have lied about why you needed his address.

Somehow it didn't occur to me. I'm a terrible liar.

That's true. Darling Bella.

I'm good at keeping secrets.

I know that.

Anyway, he came back after a fortnight, when I'd given up. I'd told myself I'd got it wrong, he didn't want to be with me and had taken the coward's way out. When he turned up forlorn, knocking on my door with an enormous bunch of flowers, I was so relieved, I knew immediately that I was completely in love with him and had no hope of giving him up. I should have been angry but I didn't have it in me.

He walked right back into your bedroom, in other words.

In other words.

I can't blame you. He's very attractive.

It wasn't just that. I knew he was the man I wanted to marry. And we did, not too long after.

Did he do the disappearing act again?

Once, when Georgie was two months old. Only for three days. I was angry with him, then.

Men get jealous of babies.

Perhaps it was that. I don't think it was, somehow. I think he checks out, when life overtakes him. I stayed in bed with Georgie while he was gone, and in some ways I rather loved it. It was easier without him there, fussing and checking what I needed, or asking if the baby was asleep yet and what was for supper. I simply enjoyed her.

You are adorable.

After three days, the telephone rang and it was David, telling me that he had been walking around and looking at the blossom and the sunshine, thinking how marvellous life was and how much he loved me and the baby.

He didn't explain where he'd slept for those nights? You didn't ask?

I didn't. I should have, but I didn't. I wanted him to come home and that was all I wanted. I didn't think knowing where he'd been or what he'd been doing would make me feel any better and could make me feel a great deal worse. So I left it.

Goodness. He does get away with it, with you.

Don't you do that with Alex?

Darling, Alex is so dependable he'd never so much as go around the corner without a fully typed-up schedule in advance telling me his movements and who to telephone if he didn't return on the dot. I long for him to give me a reason to unleash some fury but he's the goodie and I'm the baddie.

Bet you unleash the fury anyway.

Of course. But why do you think David has gone now?

I don't know. Everything has been fine. There were the usual bumps in the road but nothing we haven't had a million times before.

Perhaps he doesn't feel the same.

How can I know? He doesn't tell me.

Do you ask?

No.

No, who does? Especially if one doesn't want to know the answer. He's not working, is he?

No, he hasn't had anything for – I can't remember. Too long.

That might be it, then.

I suppose so. And poor Georgie, he didn't tell her that he'd be suddenly gone and she keeps asking me where he is and when he's coming back. I don't know what to tell her. I've got so much work on, too. I could kill him.

I don't think you should be there when he gets back.

But I don't know when he'll be home.

You need to leave the house. Alex is down at his father's place – Charlie and I were going to go down there for a while. The children are off school for a few more weeks. Come with us, it's very pretty there. You'll get inspiration for your painting.

Do you mean it?

Of course I mean it.

Won't Alex's father mind?

No, we hardly see him, he's rather retiring, relies on Alex to jolly him along. He won't mind at all. Pack a bag, come over as soon as you can. We can get the train after lunch.

Should I leave a note for David?

No. He can be as much in the dark as you were. Silly sod. I mean David, not you.

I know. Thank you, Kate. I think we will do that. Georgie would like it. I can bring my paints?

Yes, there's a room you can work in; it's got big windows, lots of light. The children can play together; there's a garden and fields all around. I would love it, to have you there. We can drink gin and talk into the small hours together.

Yes.

Yes?

Yes. Give me an hour, we'll be with you.

Good. And don't leave a note for that rascal husband of yours.

I won't.

Oh, Bella. It'll be like the old days again.

Yes, perhaps it will.

13

After only a day or two in fresh surroundings, Bella felt herself expand. She was given a bedroom of her own, at the top of the house, with two tall windows that overlooked the garden. The walls were pale blue, the bed linen pure white and the sun shone directly onto her pillow at eight o'clock, waking her. The blindness from that first morning light helped her forget things, momentarily, and she was grateful for that. They had been there several days already and still there was no news of David. There were no parents to telephone. The only family she had ever known of was a distant cousin who left David some money in his will, dead four years previously. She knew David's absence was deliberate. At unexpected moments, walking down the stairs, say, or glancing up from her book, she would remember that her husband had left her without warning or explanation, that there had been utter silence from him since, and she would be paralysed by the fright that he was dead, or dying, or lying bereft somewhere, wondering why she wasn't doing more to find him. But it would pass quickly, and she knew he was gone and would come back when he was ready. So there was fury, too.

Mostly, Bella kept herself busy, which wasn't too difficult, even in such comfortable surroundings. She would rise slowly, bathing and dressing at a pace she hadn't enjoyed since before her marriage, then go down the stairs to join the children for breakfast. (Kate would come down even later, after reading the newspaper and drinking tea in bed. Alex and his father were generally up and about early, seeing to unspecified things.) Georgie and Charlie were sleeping in adjacent rooms and were learning to become playmates. Bella knew that Georgie believed herself to be patronising Charlie, indulging in a friendship with a boy almost two years younger than her, but they both enjoyed running around the garden and cycling down the lanes.

After two cups of coffee with hot milk, and bread with butter and jam, or a four-minute boiled egg, Bella went to the room on the ground floor in which she had set up her paints and an easel. There was little else in there: an undersized armchair; a table large enough to balance a glass of water and some books; a fire grate filled with dried flowers that had long lost their colour and scent; a worn-out red rug. Crucially, there were French windows leading into the garden and a round side window. The light mostly came in the afternoon, so Bella would sketch her ideas before lunch, then paint afterwards. She had three commissions to fulfil, and the idea of an exhibition pressing upon her, too. A gallery that sold her work had expressed an interest in a show of her work, said they had a slot available in seven months' time. She would need to paint consistently if she was to manage it, but if she didn't allow herself to be too distracted by David's absence, she

114

should be able to do it. Kate came to the rescue there, too. She commissioned a portrait of Randall – due to arrive soon – as a surprise for Alex and which Bella could include in the show. Two birds killed with one stone, Kate said, and Bella winced: it was an idiom she'd never liked.

Bella saw her daughter at lunch, sometimes for a picnic. Kate would be there, too, with Charlie. Alex and his father were absent in the day, doing things outside that were never entirely specified but which seemed to make them both red-faced and pleasingly puffed-out by the evening.

A few minutes after Bella heard the grandfather clock in the hall strike six, Kate would come in to the 'studio' with two gin and tonics. These were always perfectly made with cold, fizzing tonic water, a generous number of ice cubes, a slice of lemon and a note of Angostura bitters that pleasantly hit the back of Bella's throat. Kate sometimes placed on the tray a delicate china dish of salted nuts, depending on how thin – or not – she was feeling that day.

In anticipation, Bella learned to nip quickly up the stairs to brush her hair and daub scent behind her ears, on her wrists and in the dip between her breasts. She'd slick an almost translucent red gloss on her lips but nothing else. Her skin was clear, the lines only showed when she laughed, and the sunshine she was getting in the middle of the day gave her a healthy look to belie the anguish that pressed behind her eyes in the dead of night.

14

∞

That's a pretty dress, Kate.

Thank you. It was a bit of a naughty treat to myself just before we left London.

It looks expensive. It flatters your figure.

My unfashionable hips and bosom?

That's not what I said.

I know, you're too sweet to say it. But it's what I say. Anyway, who cares? I don't get any complaints, let's say.

Alex is clearly still enthralled to you, it's rather touching to see.

Yes, he is. But I didn't mean Alex.

Oh?

Do you want another gin and tonic?

Not yet, and don't change the subject. Who did you mean?

No one. Not as such. You know how I am.

I do, which is why I'm asking.

I need a little flirtation, that's all. It keeps things ticking over, doesn't it?

I'm no good at flirting.

I think you are, Bella-moo.

What? Why?

I saw the way you were dancing at the party—

That wasn't flirting.

Did I press a nerve there?

Stop it, Kate. Who were you talking about, ticking things over for you?

Very well. He's someone I knew a long time ago, and we bumped into each other—

Bumped?

Yes, in a manner of speaking, it was on the street. He saw me first and came over to say hello.

Did you remember him?

Of course. He wasn't my first love quite but . . .

Close enough?

Yes.

Oh, Katie. You need to be so careful.

Kate put her drink down. Bella worried about it leaving a water mark and reminded herself it was not her house, not her table. The sun had started to lower, the light coming in was the yellow of dandelions on the lawn.

There's no danger. We met for a cup of coffee a few days later.

When was this?

A month or so ago.

What's his story? Go back further than that, tell me about the first time around.

I was nineteen, he was – is – three or four years older. It goes some way back because I've known him more or less all my life. Our families went on holiday to the same place, by the sea. I knew his sister better, or rather, I was in awe of her glamour. I was too shy to talk to her but I used to love watching her. I don't think I mentioned him to you before, when we were younger, I mean, because I can't remember being terribly aware of him much, until the summer I was old enough to be at the same parties as him.

And then he noticed you.

I made him notice me.

118

Yes, that sounds like the Kate I know . . . that was why I got so upset about Peter, you know. The power was all in your hands.

Not that again. We were seventeen. It's such a long time ago.

I know.

It was only a—

Truly, Kate, don't try and justify it now. I'm over it. Tell me more about . . . what is his name?

John.

John?

Yes.

Too bland for the likes of you.

His name doesn't matter.

Fine. Go on, then. What happened the summer you made him notice you?

Ha, well, the usual, I suppose. We danced, we kissed. I thought I'd fallen in love. Writing his name out and imagining our children. Drawing wedding dresses.

Did it last longer than the summer?

It always ended when we went home, but we would pick up again the next year. That happened for three summers. And then one year he didn't come back.

Did you know why?

He married Elaine.

What? The girl who—

Yes, the one with the garden.

It was her party where—

Yes, exactly there. They didn't meet by the sea but at work – a funny coincidence, though they probably never even realised they had me in common. At any rate, it seems his family weren't too keen on her and she preferred to spend her summers abroad.

So you hadn't seen him for twenty years until a month ago?

No.

Had you thought about him?

Off and on, over the years, as you do. I'd wondered what he would be like now.

What *is* he like now?

Still married.

Ah.

Unhappily.

They always say that.

Maybe because it's true. Elaine was a bit of a bitch, wasn't she?

I don't really remember. Is he still good-looking?

How do you know he was good-looking in the
first place?

You only do good-looking.

You make me sound predictable. But yes, he is. He's
classically handsome, even. And he's worn it well with
age. Bella, you mustn't repeat any of this to Alex.

I wouldn't dream of it. Have they met?

Slightly. He came to our last party.

The one I was at?

Yes.

You run close to the wire.

Up to that point, there wasn't anything to worry about.

Something happened? Elaine wasn't there, was she?

No, he came on his own. I don't know what excuse
he gave. In theory nothing happened but . . . there
was a tension. I knew that if I'd wanted something to
happen, it could have.

So you didn't want it to?

I did, very much. In that moment. We found ourselves
alone, in the hall.

What stopped you?

I knew I'd had too much to drink, that I wasn't
thinking straight. And there was you.

Me?

I knew you'd disapprove.

Don't make *me* the moral arbiter, Kate. I don't stand on any higher ground.

OK. Truthfully, it wasn't that so much. Your disapproval, that is.

Bella was curled up on a chair, her hands clasped between her thighs. The drinks were long finished, and she heard the clock strike seven. Soon, the children would need their supper.

I'm not quite sure what to say.

There's nothing to say. It was only that I think I knew I didn't want anything to get in the way of us becoming friends again.

Yes. I feel the same.

I know how I am, Bella. I'll start something with a man and it takes up all my time.

You're married already.

See! I knew you would disapprove.

I'm not making any judgement—

Yes, you are.

Kate. I'm *your* friend, I'm listening to you. But from where I'm standing, Alex looks like a good man.

He is a good man.

So why would you have an affair?

Not so loudly! I won't. I just wanted to feel wanted again. Don't you miss that? The anticipation, the waiting and the wondering.

I'd like my husband back, most of all. I am not enjoying the waiting and the wondering at all.

No.

I only want to know where he is and when he's coming back.

Is there no one you can telephone?

I spoke to the police yesterday – I couldn't stand it any longer.

You didn't tell me that.

I'm telling you now. Anyway, it was no good. They said they would take down his description and details but as he is a healthy adult – so far as I know – he is likely to have left of his own accord. Even if they found him, they couldn't force him to come back to me. I knew all this already, from before. I don't know why I bothered.

You had to do something.

Yes, I suppose that was it.

How long has it been now?

Eleven days. Georgie asks where he is every night and I don't have an answer for her. I can only say 'soon'. It makes me so angry. Half of me doesn't even want him to come back because I don't think I trust myself not to strangle him with my bare hands if he does.

You don't think he's gone because of what happened at the party?

What do you mean?

Darling Bella. You can't think none of us noticed.

What? What did you notice?

The way you were with—

You gave me that blue pill. Most of it is a blur. I danced, that was all.

Yes, but you looked very close. Perhaps David saw, and was jealous.

Do you *know* if David saw? Kate, tell me – did he say anything to you?

Not as such. I caught his eye, nothing more than that.

Oh God. Nothing happened. Nothing I wanted. Nothing I meant. He came up to me, we weren't introduced. He was there, and . . .

The coldness of that floor, the whiteness of the tiles.

. . . then he wasn't.

Don't cry, Bella. I'm so sorry. I shouldn't have started this conversation.

No, it's not what you're saying. It's because I know David has left me.

He's thinking things over, that's all. I'm sure he'll be back.

How can you be sure?

I know it, that's all. Trust in me. Dry your eyes, let's go through. The children will be wrecking the place and we need another drink. Darling? What is it? You've gone pale.

15

Bella learned how the light came into the room at different hours. She put the chair in the right spot for the morning sun. The angle of her easel was adjusted. The canvas set upon it and secured. This was a chance to do what she knew she was good at: watching, absorbing, understanding and recreating. Only this time, she would look inside her mind. Other people often made the mistake of thinking that her best portraits were of those she knew and loved. It was true that there were a few drawings and even one painting of Georgie that she was proud of; she had caught the tilt of her daughter's chin, the repose in which her thoughtfulness and sensitivity were best drawn out. With great love she had carefully mixed the colours for her skin, her hair, her lips. Technically, there was a precision in that painting that she had not always done so well before. Yet it did not represent to her the real challenge of her work. It proved nothing to her of her ability.

This would be her masterpiece.

To paint someone whom she both loathed and did

not know. Sometimes, she was not certain even of his existence.

As she recalled the lines that made him, she would discover the answer. She would paint him, know him, own him.

16

Although the house was in the country, surrounded by fields that lay flat end to end, all the way to the horizon, there seemed to be a never-ending stream of people coming through the doors. Parcels were delivered, milk left on the doorstep, someone came to unblock the drain, another to drop by a key or return a borrowed ladder. There were men who worked in the garden, women who mended curtains, children who came around to play with Charlie. Alex and his father were glimpsed but rarely amongst this crowd yet were presumably directing their movements, conductors of their pace. Kate seemed unperturbed by the apparent strangers who walked into a room and immediately set about a task, with no acknowledgement made on either side. Bella couldn't feel the same. Someone else close by, whether silently engaged in whatever they were doing or not, shifted the dynamic in ways she felt disturbed by. Her senses were too heightened. She didn't know if it was because she didn't have David at her side and felt the gaping chasm of emptiness surrounding her at all hours, or whether it was because she wasn't in her own house and had no knowledge of what those distant, small sounds might be. She kept finding herself jumping at ridiculous things – a knock, a bell, a scrape.

In her makeshift studio, at least, she was far enough at the end of the house to have no one walking through it and everyone seemed to understand that this space had been given over to her and her alone. So it was a jolt when Kate walked in with Randall, for his first sitting, even more so because they entered as stealthily as if they were casing the joint for a robbery.

Here's the boy wonder.

Bella's back faced the door and she turned quickly, thankful the paintbrush was not in her hand at that moment or she would have scarred the canvas. Randall did not greet Bella but walked to the chair that sat opposite her easel, bathed in the afternoon sunshine, and sat down in it.

I'm ready.

Before Bella could find the words to reply, Kate had gripped her by the arm.

Remember, not a word to Alex. It's our secret.

How long is it going to take?

Flustered, Bella tried to pull herself together.

I usually ask for three or four sittings. It depends really on how much I manage each time.

You are a marvel, darling. Enjoy getting to know each other.

Kate kissed Bella, and left. Randall remained, an amused look on his face. He nodded at his parting stepmother.

Yes. We will.

17

Bella, I forgot to say, there's a dinner tonight.

Here?

Yes, Alex's father has invited some people over. I'm not quite sure who. Usual suspects, probably.

Who are the usual suspects?

Oh, neighbours, people he's known for years. They're all perfectly nice. Not too exciting, so I thought . . .

What did you think? I can see the mischief in your eyes.

I thought it would be more fun if I mixed things up a bit. Alex has some old friends from round here, and I put in a call to one or two of them.

Why do I get the feeling that Alex wouldn't be pleased about this?

He will be when they get here. It's not that they're not his friends, it's more that . . . well, one has a very unsuitable, much younger girlfriend. And the other is married to a woman he loathes.

Is that going to make for a fun evening?

Once everyone's had a few drinks, I'm sure it will.

I didn't bring anything to wear.

You can borrow something of mine, I've got plenty of things here.

I've got a black dress – perhaps you could lend me a necklace, to pretty it up a bit.

Of course. Why don't we get ready together? Like we did when we were younger? We can spend hours in the bath and then paint our nails. I'll dry your hair for you.

What about the children?

I've arranged for a girl in the village to come and give them supper, put them to bed. We can relax and enjoy ourselves. Come on, Bella. I think it would do you good.

When we spent hours getting ready at seventeen, it was because we couldn't decide what to wear and we were talking endlessly about the boys we would see that night. I'm not sure that trying to hide my grey hairs and finding a pair of shoes that don't make my feet ache gives one quite the same pre-party sensation.

Honestly, Bella. You'll talk yourself into old age before your time if you're not careful. We're in our early forties. These are our prime years!

Are they?

Yes, they are. These are the years when we know ourselves best.

The years when we have to watch what we eat.

Or, the years when we know what clothes flatter. Not to mention when we know what we want in bed, and we're not afraid to ask for it.

I don't know about that. I'm quite shy.

Even with David, after all these years?

Who else would I be shy with? Yes, even with David.

Lights off?

Not quite. I mean, we have fun in bed. It gets better, the longer you've been together, don't you think? I'm just not good at asking for specifics.

You think good girls don't ask, but boys like a bad girl in bed.

I was taught they liked them but they didn't marry them.

And I don't know about the longer together bit, either. Don't you miss the electricity of the new lover? The sudden spark that sets off sensations in parts of your body you'd forgotten you had?

You've invited that man, haven't you?

What?

Kate. The man you said something almost happened with. At your party. Don't be obtuse, you know exactly who I mean.

Yes, all right. I might have done.

He's coming all this way?

It turns out that he had to be this way for something else.

How handy. What is it he has to be this way for?

Some work thing.

A made-up thing.

Bella, don't be like that with me. You're my only friend. If I can't talk to you about it, I'll go mad.

Hmm.

I didn't encourage him, I promise you. And nothing has happened yet. We were talking on the telephone—

You're calling each other?

Not often. Don't look at me like that. He said he could easily find an excuse to be here, and the next thing I know, he's gone and done it. I feel terrible about it, I do – you must believe me. I can't stop him.

Why not?

He's crazy about me. I honestly think if I don't let him come down he'll do something much more dangerous.

Tell me the truth, Kate.

I always do.

Are you in love with him?

No, I don't think so. I could be. Sometimes, I think I'd like to be. But I don't want to leave Alex, and I don't want Alex leaving me.

Then what is going on with John?

Shh. Not so loud.

You're the one asking me to keep your secrets, Kate. I know how to be quiet.

I know. I'm talking to you about it not because I want you to keep secrets for me . . . that is, I do. But only because he's forced me into this situation. Nothing has happened yet, remember.

Yet. A very telling word.

It's not Alex's fault but he doesn't make me feel the same way. John makes me feel good about myself again. I didn't think men wanted me any more. I don't get looked at in the street like I used to. I stopped traffic when I was younger.

I know, I saw it.

Do you know how depressing it is not to get that attention any more? I feel invisible. I'm only asking for a teensy enjoyable flirtation.

It doesn't sound as if this man is happy to leave it at that, though. You're playing with fire, Kate. Not to mention you are the least invisible woman I know.

Don't make such a thing of it. There will be several – *several* – other people there. Alex will hardly notice him.

Don't put him next to you at the dinner.

I won't. I'll go one better. I'll put him next to you.

All the better to see his teeth.

All the better for him to see yours.

18

At five o'clock, as arranged, Bella went to Kate's room. She knew Kate was in a fever of anticipation for the night ahead, experiencing that delicious hope for the unforeseen. Reality had not yet set its limits. Bella could not help but remember this feeling as being so much the sweeter when they were younger and more innocent, less knowing of the disappointments. A time before men at a party talked about which was the best route to take from here to there or discussed with heightened enthusiasm the pros and cons of different pieces of expensive sports equipment or car mechanics. A time before women asked you coded questions about your husband's work, what school your children went to or where your house was, in order to ascertain into which box they could lock you away. A time before the need to hold in your stomach when someone glanced down, or hoped food wasn't stuck between your teeth, or wished you could interrupt the flow of a dynamic conversation about the peccadillos of a movie star with a question about the best pills to take for water retention because someone mentioned garden hoses.

And she could see how Kate was deep diving into the idea of the love affair if only to snatch at that youthful state of blurred vision. The problem was, it threw the harsh lines of Bella's current state of mind into even sharper relief. But she was determined to try, to have this moment with her friend.

Bella knocked and Kate called out for her to come in. The room had windows on two walls, the pale shades of the nearing violet dusk visible outside. The curtains were not drawn but she had turned on the low table lamps and lit a candle. There was a heavy scent of tuberose in the room. Three different dresses were laid out on the bed: black, silver and white. Kate's 'colours'. Kate sat at the dressing table, wrapped in an oyster-coloured silk gown, brushing back her dark hair. There was a triptych mirror and a number of bottles filled with liquids and lotions. Draped on the mirror were several necklaces. Before it was a glass cube of make-up brushes standing alongside smaller trinkets: a tiny china pot with two lovebirds, a large gold die, a matchbox covered in seed pearls, a glass painted figurine. Georgie had described all of these things to Bella earlier, after a happy hour or so let loose on Kate's powders and lipsticks.

Two crystal tumblers filled with ice, lemon, gin and tonic. Kate picked one up and handed it to Bella as she came in.

Bella was wearing her plain black dress. It fitted her well, she knew that, at least. She had shaved her legs and put on burgundy silk knickers and bra, the best she owned. There was the potential risk that Kate would offer to lend her another dress, persuade her to try it on, and she didn't want Kate to see her in underwear that was off-white and unflattering, the things she usually put on in the morning. Bella wondered at herself, why she didn't throw away those items that made her feel shabby. Sometimes she pretended she didn't care, though she always did. If she was someone who could be good to herself she would chuck them but that seemed somehow profligate and vain. This constant balancing act between pleasing others, pleasing frugality and pleasing her secret desires was one of the more exhausting aspects of grown-up life. This occurred to Bella as she crossed the room in her bare feet and stretched out her hand to receive the cool glass.

Kate looked enchanting.

Age-old insecurities gripped Bella by the throat. When rational she felt, on the whole, that the years had been good to her. In fact, she was one of the few who believed she was better-looking now than when she was a girl of sixteen, with a plump chin and bad clothes. Since their reunion, Kate had been generous to her, too, telling her that she was a magnificent creature. Nor could she fault David, who would compliment her when they were going out and, though he never noticed anything like a new haircut, could be relied upon to give frank and helpful remarks on her outfit, if asked. There were days when Bella could look in the mirror and believe herself to be more than the sum of her unremarkable parts. But she photographed badly, and had ruined plenty of evenings for herself by catching a glimpse of her silhouette in a window or mirror as she walked past, seeing only the bump in her nose or a forehead that was too high. An aunt had once told her that the two of them shared a lack of beauty that others might pity but she was not to worry because 'the men that fancy us, *really* do'. It hadn't provided much comfort.

Kate held a thin gold chain up to her neck, from which hung a single stone, the blue of Aegean seas. A present from Alex on her last birthday. Bella knew Kate's skin felt like velvet to the touch, her hair was glossy, even her nails grew fast and strong. Bella had flicked through the albums downstairs – Kate and Alex's wedding, family summer holidays – and knew there was no such thing as a bad photograph of her old friend. Kate had access to an easy confidence in her own powers of attraction that lit a small fire of jealousy in Bella, in spite of the caveat that Kate feared growing old in a way that she did not. Maybe it was only because she had less to lose but it didn't feel like an advantage.

Bella took the drink and sat on the edge of the bed, watching Kate's reflection in the mirror, like Snow White's stepmother. Their eyes met, and their lips smiled in unison. Whatever Kate asked Bella to do on this evening, she would be complicit in her crimes and she was powerless to prevent it.

19

At the dinner, a long narrow table was set with candles and short-stemmed yellow roses in doll-sized vases. Each end of the table seemed to stretch to a vanishing point and Bella felt dizzied at the idea of counting how many people there were. Then she would turn her head and see Alex or his father sitting at either end as close as if they had pushed forwards on gliding chairs. Bile threatened to rise in her throat, and she clutched a glass of cold water as if it were a rock on the seabed. Her head throbbed from a stabbing pain behind her eyes. There were painkillers in her bathroom upstairs and after the cheese had been served she would excuse herself to fetch them; to do so now risked drawing attention to herself. Kate would disapprove of Bella getting up before the dinner was over. In the meantime, she must steel herself to participate, to watch what was going on. She had a task to complete.

Opposite Bella sat Kate, in the silver dress she had changed into at the last minute, shimmering like a desert mirage. To Bella's right sat John and on her left was a man who had greeted her politely before he turned his attention to the woman on his other side and never looked back. Also opposite her, three chairs along from Kate, sat Randall. Though Bella was not looking directly at him, she knew he was silent and watching her. She was not frightened by him but his gaze unsettled her. The day before, when Randall was sitting for her, she had asked him an innocuous question about his school years. He had responded by asking if he might light a cigarette, and she saw the tremor in his hands. They were not, he had said, his best years.

It gave her a shard of power, to feel pity for those who had harmed him but not forgiveness. For him, for all mankind.

Bella adjusted her body towards John. It wasn't hard to see why Kate found him tempting. He smiled at Bella, showing a set of even teeth as if he were shining a torch onto her face.

With surprising warmth, John introduced himself and asked her name. She told him and they asked each other the usual warm-up questions, a knockabout tennis rally. She established that she was an old friend of Kate's, recently reunited, and that she did not know Alex so well, but he had been very generous in having both her and her daughter to stay. (She did not mention that she, too, had known his wife when they were young.) Her husband would be joining them soon, she added. She didn't know why. Some generic fear of being misidentified as single.

He said, how funny, he too had known Kate a long time ago and had recently been reunited with her by chance. He happened to be in the area for a work thing – he did not specify what – and was able to join the dinner. He did not mention Elaine, and Bella did not ask if he was married. There was no ring.

Already she was complicit in their secret. Bella knew that

142

it would please Kate and John, bond them closer. And make turning back even harder.

All around them the chatter was lively, the wine was poured, the food was served. Bella picked at her plate, chewing more air than food, but John was polite enough not to comment.

When the next course was served, Bella looked to her left but it seemed the man on that side had no intention of turning around to talk to her. She glanced back at John, and saw the woman on his other side was firmly facing away. They caught each other's eyes.

Looks like you're stuck with me.

Bella laughed. The pain had started to ease a little, the light in the room felt less glaring. John grabbed a bottle and poured more wine into her glass, and into his.

Neither of us has to drive – we may as well, don't you think?

Something in the way he looked at her when he said this made Bella glance at Kate, who seemed to feel the two of them regard her. She turned, raised her glass a touch and tipped her head to the side as she acknowledged them both.

20

Randall watched you all throughout the dinner.

He did?

Yes, I could see him. He seems a little besotted by you.

I doubt it very much.

Why? I know that look in the eyes of men.

Kate, please.

You shouldn't doubt so easily that a young man could be in love with you.

I'm not—

You are. But you're beautiful, Bella. I don't know why you don't see it.

Thank you. Let's not have this conversation now, though.

Why not? We're in our best years, we should enjoy them. It'll speed past us soon enough and we'll be shrivelled hags being wheeled out to the garden by nurses, wishing we'd had more sex when it was on offer.

Charming. Speak for yourself, old hag.

The point is, Randall—

Kate, he's your stepson.

Exactly. He's not my son, it's not the same.

If you keep doing this to me, I shall have to bring up the subject of John.

Did he mention me?

You know he did.

Do you think he's keen?

Undoubtedly. Are you going to do something about it?

No. I won't. I know I shouldn't, and I won't.

So there you go. Neither of us is going to do anything we shouldn't.

All right, Bella. You win. I'll be a good girl this time.

21

My darling Bella,

I know I don't deserve to say this, but I have been going out of my mind with worry. I didn't know where you were. I came home three days ago and you had gone, with Georgie. No note, nothing. I saw the cases had gone, your toothbrush, Bearly from Georgie's bed. I couldn't think where you might be, and no one I knew to ask had any idea either. Not Jenny, nor Charlotte. Stupidly, it only occurred to me this morning to ask at Kate's house and someone there, a gardener I think, said that she was away. Luckily, he knew the address. I am writing now in the hope that this finds you. I miss you terribly. Please come home.

Your loving husband,
David

22

No apology?

No. He doesn't say sorry at all.

Bloody cheek of it.

I don't think he even realises that he did the same to me, but worse.

How can he not realise?

I think something happens to his mind that either blanks everything else out, or somehow justifies it. He believes he needs to disappear, and that we need to understand that. If he said sorry that would mean facing up to the fact that he has done something wrong, and he isn't strong enough for that.

You're very calm about it.

I'm not. I just don't know how else to be. And Georgie can't have me falling to pieces.

Have you written back?

Not yet.

Will you?

Yes, probably. I don't feel like doing it straight away.

No. Don't go home yet, Bella.

No.

I'm not going to tell you what to do with your marriage but I want you to stay here a little longer. There's still so much we need to do together.

Is there?

Yes, there's so much more talking I want to do. And then there's your work.

Yes.

The portrait of Randall—

Yes, he's quite a patient sitter.

I wonder who looks at the other the most.

What do you mean?

Well, you have to study him to paint him. But he likes to look at you, as we've seen.

Don't start all that again.

Only teasing. Alex worries about him. Randall doesn't seem to know what he wants to do with his life. He's only here to teach Charlie how to shoot, and Alex is paying him for the lessons. He doesn't see how unhelpful that is.

Isn't it better that Alex pays him for a job done, rather than just giving him handouts?

Yes, but he should go out to earn a wage in a real job. He's had plenty of handouts, too. I don't know, I've never been able to get through to him. I bet you would do much better.

I don't see why.

I'm the wicked stepmother, there's no hope for me. And Alex isn't aware of it but some of his son's behaviour towards me can be very odd.

Odd, how?

Once he caught me as I was coming out of my bedroom. He was walking past my doorway, on his way from the bathroom presumably, with nothing but a tiny towel wrapped around his waist.

That's just bad timing, isn't it?

He barely held onto the towel, Bella. And he kept me there, talking, for quite a while. I had to fix my eyes on his face but it was quite difficult.

Kate, I—

I'm not asking for sympathy. I only mean to say, it's quite bizarre, isn't it?

Yes, I suspect it is.

It's transfixing, somehow. It's probably some sort of jealousy with his father. Oedipal complex, sort of thing.

Yes. Perhaps that.

Not that I would do anything. But it plays on your mind. Should I tell Alex?

How would he react?

No, you're right. I couldn't. It would only mean the most terrific row. I'll leave it alone. Let's not talk about it any more. What were we talking about before?

The letter I had from David.

Oh, darling, I'm so sorry. Of course, I shouldn't have started talking about . . . Yes, so what will you do?

I'm going to think about it for a little longer before I respond. I'm still angry.

Angry enough to leave him?

No, I don't want to do that. But I can't go back to things as they were. We have to work it out, somehow. We can, can't we?

Will you ask him why he left, not to mention why he went without telling you he was going?

I shall have to. I doubt he'll have an answer, though.

Why don't you ask him down here?

What?

Yes, ask him down here. Then you can see him on your territory—

It's not my territory.

It is, so far as he's concerned. You're my friend. If he comes here he'll have to be on the lookout.

What, in case you jump out at him from behind a door?

In a way. The point is, it would mean that you weren't answering to his beck and call, but he could answer to yours, for once.

I'm not a complete pushover.

I'm sure you're not, my sweet. But you need to take control of this situation.

My marriage isn't a *situation*.

Are you going to fight with me about this, or with David?

No, sorry. I'm on edge but not because of you. I'll think about it but thank you for the offer. Perhaps we had better check with Alex first?

Why? He'll do as I ask. There's plenty of room.

All right, in that case, yes, thank you. We *do* appreciate being here. Georgie is having a happy time. She and Charlie are getting on well.

Aren't they? It's good for Charlie to have a friend down here. They're hatching a plot to build a den in the garden today, apparently. Georgie seems willing to pitch in.

Yes, she doesn't mind getting her hands dirty. I love seeing her come in with muddy knees. Granny never let me get a speck on my clothes without a ticking off.

No, they didn't then.

That's true. Katie, do you think everything will be all right?

Of course it will.

I didn't think marriage would be like this, not at this stage, when we've been married for so long. I thought it would get easier.

The only thing I know for certain is that nothing in life turns out the way you think it will. Let's go and find the children and take them for a walk, then we can come back and have supper in the garden.

Yes, let's. Thank you for all that you do for me.

I like to do it. I'm on your side, Bella.

I know.

23

Bella waited one further day, not two, before she wrote back to David. Only – she told herself – because she didn't want another night's disturbed sleep, playing out an argument with him over and over. It certainly wasn't to ease *his* state of mind. In the short letter, she made no apology of her own and said that if he wanted to see Georgie he could come down to the house. They would talk then. She didn't make it clear whether or not he would be welcome to stay overnight; she wasn't sure if she would want that, or not. Bella knew she did not want to end her marriage but she did want the current state of play to end. She wondered if he was ill, and then whether thinking that was because she was trying to excuse him in some way. To end thoughts of him, Bella went to look for Georgie.

She found her daughter sitting by a window on the first floor, overlooking a courtyard. It was bare but for grass that grew between the cracks, and two large terracotta pots of an indistinguishable green plant with brown tips on the long leaves. Clouds thickly covered the sky like seafoam but the light was bright enough. Bella stroked her daughter's hair and curled up beside her.

What are you looking at out there?

Georgie nudged her small, warm body closer to her mother's, and nodded her head to the right. Bella saw Charlie, holding a shotgun. One eye squinted, the other was focused with serious intent upon a carefully stacked pyramid of empty cans. Beside him stood Randall, tousled hair and crumpled shirt. His arm was at an angle that gave her a shock of recognition, or perhaps it was déjà vu. She could see his lips moving, his stare fixed upon the target.

Silently, they continued to watch, jolting mildly when Charlie pulled the trigger and a loud bang sounded, just as the pyramid went down.

Charlie doesn't shoot rabbits, Mummy. Not yet.

Bella smiled, to reassure her daughter that she knew there was no serious danger.

And she thought: if only the gun that Charlie held in his hand was the most dangerous weapon a man could have.

Can I have a go?

Georgie's face was tilted up to her mother's. They felt close, loving. Bella felt a wash of guilt that she had not been paying enough attention to her daughter lately. Her line of vision had been filled with Kate, and David, and— She stopped herself. Instead, she bent down and kissed Georgie's nose, wrapped her arms around her. Delighted, Georgie kissed her back and stretched her arms around Bella. They inhaled each other, and giggled. Bella stole a glance through the window again, and saw Randall's hand touching Charlie on the shoulder, steadying him as he gave instructions.

She closed her eyes and waited for the jolt to pass.

No, he would not be teaching her daughter.

Sorry, darling.

Georgie gave a nod. Bella knew her daughter's impulse was to say it was unfair, she was older than Charlie, why shouldn't she learn how to shoot and was it because she was a girl? But she also knew Georgie did not want to disturb this state of intimacy with an argument. Nor did Bella. There was a pull to return home, where they had their routines and the comfort of familiarity. Georgie, she knew, was bewildered by their stay with Kate. There was never a clear answer on where her father was, the food was different, she missed her own bed, her books and toys. It wasn't a proper holiday and no one had said when they would be going back. And yet, Bella wasn't ready to give the answers she knew her daughter needed and she had to hold onto the belief that if David came down here, that would be her best chance of having it out with him (whatever 'it' was). And then they could begin again, laying the foundations for a family life that would keep them steady for years to come. Replacing the straw house with bricks.

She had to hold on.

Bella took her daughter's hand and pulled her up. There was another gunshot and Bella laughed, dispersing in herself and for her daughter, the fear created by the sudden noise.

They walked down the stairs together and out through the front door, down the path and onto the lane, their fingers still laced together. Georgie gave a half-skip step every now and then to keep pace with her mother, chatting lightly about her favourite spots as they walked past them. The place where the fattest raspberries grew, the corner where a boy had come whizzing past on his bicycle, the house that had creepy upstairs windows. Bella made noises of encouragement as she wondered at the courage of her little girl, who had endeavoured to explore and conquer this unknown space, making it known to her. They walked until Georgie said she was feeling hungry and she'd been told there would be mashed potatoes at supper tonight, her favourite, so they had better get back. And they did.

24

∞

In the night, sometimes, she remembered lying there. How cold it was.

25

Where have Charlie and Georgie gone?

Just over there. They're lying down on the riverbank, that's why you can't see them. I think they're trying to tickle trout.

Sweet. It's a gorgeous day, isn't it?

Yes, so warm. It's tricking us into believing summer won't be over soon.

Here, have a glass of this. It's not too sticky.

Thank you. Kate, do you ever think of staying here?

What? All the time?

Yes.

Hmm. Sometimes. Charlie loves it here so much, the freedom to run around. Alex is not too different, really. He's made for tramping about in the mud all day then sitting by a fire at night. I think I would miss the city, but then one gets so exhausted by all the goings on.

Georgie has had a very happy time – I do have to thank you and Alex for that. It's partly what's made me wonder.

About not going back?

In a way. I know it's idyllic when it looks like this . . .

Yes, it's a different story in the winter when the snow blocks you in and everyone's slipping and sliding down hills.

Of course. But it's the fact of it being so easy here that I love so much. I don't feel as if I'm negotiating all the time, trading off my energy for things that one loathes to get done.

Yes, the list of things to do is smaller here. But that's in every respect – the fun things, not just the boring ones.

You say that but how often do you go to exhibitions or admire the architecture in town?

Not enough, I admit. Not as much as I pretend I do when I justify not living here.

How are things with Alex?

The same as ever. It's not that he is anything I thought he wasn't. The one thing you can't accuse Alex of is being the wild card.

And that's exactly what you'd like him to be.

Well, yes. I know it sounds ungrateful and I don't mean to be. He's a good father, he looks after us both, and he does his best with Randall.

When did Randall last talk to his mother?

I don't know. Years, I think.

What was the problem?

Alex says she was a drinker but who knows, really? I know it must have been a shocker. Alex doesn't talk about it but I think he was very unhappy when it ended. She bolted out of the blue.

How old was he? Randall, I mean.

Six.

Poor boy.

Yes, I don't think that sort of thing leaves you without a mark. Well, you can see it for yourself. Neither of us can get through to him. Not like you can.

I don't think I can.

You have got through to him. In a way, I was amazed Randall agreed to sit for you. What has it been like?

People always think something mysterious happens in a studio but it doesn't. The person sits and I look at them and try to reproduce something of them on a canvas.

Sounds pretty mystical to me. But it's the fact of his sitting there for so long, and agreeably, that surprised me. Has he seen the painting yet?

No, I'm not certain when – or even if – I'll show it to him. If you do, that's for you to decide.

When will I be able to see it?

I don't know. Possibly not until it's finished.

How do you sell anything, Bella?

I do all right.

Darling Bella. Yes, you do. More than all right. Are you looking forward to seeing David?

I don't know. I still love him, very much. But if he doesn't explain himself this time, I think I may be too angry to go on. Sometimes I think it would be easier if it was just you and me with the children.

Yes, I think that would be heavenly, too. Look at them now, they've been getting on so well, haven't they? They're becoming more and more like brother and sister. Isn't it a nice thought, that they will still know each other in the years to come, and they'll have this history as part of them? We know what a difference that makes.

It does. Kate, perhaps we should think about it.

Are you being serious now?

I think I am. What if I didn't go back to David, but stayed here, or somewhere nearby?

A cottage with roses around the door?

Something like that, yes.

I think that sounds very romantic. And unlikely.

I don't see why not. You can grow roses anywhere.

Very funny. What do I do with Alex and his father? Wrap them up in brown paper and string, and send them back to town? Actually, that is rather tempting.

We'd have the run of the place with the children.

You could paint masterpieces, and I could . . . I'd have to think about that one. An actress needs a stage.

All the world's a stage . . .

Shame no one buys tickets to the world, that's all. Perhaps I could sell your paintings for you, bump the prices up and close the deals with my dazzling smile.

If anyone could, you could, Kate.

The truth is, everything is so much easier when we're talking. I missed you for all those years.

Did you?

I did. I needed my Bella-moo. Didn't you miss me?

I thought about you nearly every day for years. I think it was a sort of bereavement that I went through when I didn't hear from you again.

162

I was selfish. I'm so sorry.

You don't need to apologise any more, I do understand it now. Let's lie down, like we used to, and look at the clouds.

There's a house up there for us, see? There's the chimney, there's a tiny round window in the attic.

Big enough for both of us, just about.

It's cosy, not small. The children would come around to see us and we'd bake scones for them.

Very funny, Kate. You've never baked a scone in your life.

As you well know, I never say never to anything.

Hold my hand. Let's dream it for a little while, and maybe we won't wake up.

Yes, Bella. Let's.

26

Two women, lying on a blanket, on the grass. Their bodies are long, parallel and almost touching. They are holding hands gently, their fingers laced together but not gripping. Their hair is loose, their eyes are open and their lips are moving only a little. They appear to be studying the clouds, perhaps playing the child's game of making pictures in the sky.

Nearby, grass has been cut and the scent of it floats on the warm air. The flowers are on the cusp of fading. Hydrangeas are dusky pink, like faded blotting paper; rose petals curl at the edges. Unseen but not unheard are the two children, at the far end of the garden.

Tears stream from the eyes of the fair woman, though she makes no sobs, says nothing. The other props up on an elbow, their hands are undone but she puts an arm around her friend's waist. And then she bends down, slowly. They both watch each other as this happens, as if it happens by impulse, not will.

They kiss, and Randall looks away.

27

∝∞∝

Bella sat, facing him. He was seated in a position that had become a little uncomfortable for him, she could see, but he dared not move. After a few sessions together, she could read his features as easily as a nursery rhyme and understood he was trying hard to find the right words for what he wanted to say.

What he said was unexpected.

I am sorry.

Bella put her paintbrush down. She knew he must be able to see the confusion on her face. That said, whether he was able to interpret the change in her aspect, she wasn't sure. She didn't think he had the ability to empathise but now that he had said those three words, her certainty had been undermined.

Sorry for what?

Kate.

Could you tilt your chin up a touch?

Like this?

Yes. What do you mean, you are sorry for Kate. Not sorry *for* her of course – about her, I assume?

You must be disappointed that she doesn't love you as you thought she did.

What do you think you know of how we feel about each other? And is this an appropriate conversation for you to be having about your stepmother?

She means nothing to me.

I see.

I didn't need her as a mother when I first met her and I don't need her now. Which is just as well as it turns out. It was immediately clear she had no intention of being one.

Perhaps she was being careful not to tread on your mother's toes.

My mother died when I was six.

Died? I thought she—

Yes, technically she left. She left without telling me she was going and I heard nothing from her for weeks, which for a young child feels a lot longer. So far as I am concerned, she died that day.

I'm so sorry.

It's hardly your apology to make.

I'm not apologising for her. I am expressing sympathy for the sadness she caused.

There's no sadness. I never thought about her again.

I see.

I know you don't believe me. People find it hard to believe that I don't miss her, never have, but she was not a kind mother when she was here.

I would say another sentimental phrase here, but I am guessing it's not one you want to hear.

No, thank you. It's unnecessary. Shall I tell you of her cruelty?

Only if it's something you feel the need to tell me.

When I was four, she told me I was too old for kisses. There were to be no more.

You were four!

She kept her word.

You were a young child.

Yes. I'm ashamed to admit it now but I would go into her dressing room each morning, after she had left, and take from the wastepaper basket the tissue she had used to blot her lipstick. I would press it to my cheek and pretend she had kissed me.

And you say you never thought about her after she left?

Her going was a relief to us all. My father was much happier. I believe money was sent on the condition that there would be no further word. He spent more time with me after she had gone, and I liked the things we did together. He taught me how to shoot.

And he would give you kisses?

I don't remember too many but it's different for a boy with his father. I learned to be a man with him. The point I'm trying to get to is that he married the same woman again.

I don't know about that. Kate is more affectionate with Charlie than it seems your mother was with you.

Yes, she is. But does she do it from instinct or social expectation?

I think instinct. She's not so harsh as all that. She's fond of you, you know.

Hmm. Do you mind if I smoke?

Not until after I've finished. We'll take a break soon. There isn't long to go, it's nearly done.

Randall acknowledged this with silence. He kept his position, only allowing his eyes to move. As he spoke, he looked out of the window. The day was still, a cool white light.

So, are you going to respond?

To what?

To the fact that Kate doesn't love you as you thought she did.

I see no reason to respond to that, no. Why are you interested in what goes on between Kate and me, anyway?

I'm not.

Hmm. You're slouching a little, can you straighten your back, please?

It's aching, that's why.

Not much longer. I have to go and see Georgie.

I don't see why everyone should be so fascinated with my father's wife.

She's beautiful, which always helps. But she has presence, too. Star power I suppose you could call it. It makes her the centre of any room, even if she isn't switching it on. I think we're all helpless when we come into her orbit.

I think you are much more beautiful.

Very kind. But even if I were, I don't have her charisma.

Her charisma has passed me by.

So you say. Now, don't be naughty. I'm not going to be disloyal to her; you can stop your goading.

I want to kiss you, Bella.

Now—

You let Kate kiss you. You let—

I don't know what you're talking about, and I'm warning you to stop there.

You didn't see me but I saw you.

Don't do this.

No one ever notices me. I'm the ghost in the corner of the room. I used to pity myself. But then I saw it for what it was. A supernatural power.

You didn't see anything.

But I did. I walk the corridors without a sound, I slip through doorways.

You're a creep.

Yes, and you think that's an insult. Perhaps it is. But I see the truth. I hear it, too. The things that no one else sees because they are too noisy and too brash.

Randall—

Don't say my name as if you were my parent.

Randall, whatever you thought you saw—

I know I saw.

Whatever it was, you only saw one single picture. You don't know the context.

A picture tells a thousand words.

If you want to believe the cliché.

It's only a cliché because it's true.

Context still matters.

Then why do you paint portraits?

What?

A portrait is nothing more than a single moment in time of a person's life, isn't it?

Yes, but—

And yet you would say that the power of a portrait is that it can tell everything about that person in the single moment that the artist chose to capture.

Everything is open to debate.

Maybe. But isn't that the point? Isn't that what people say about your work? That you manage to convey layers of meaning and emotion in a frozen point of time.

I'm flattered if they do say that. But that portrait is painted after several hours with a sitter, as you know. It looks like a single moment, but I have only arrived at that moment after I have come to know the person, to know which particular look or pose conveys their personality. And even then, I wouldn't dream of saying that I have captured their entire sense of self. Only as much as they were prepared to reveal to me in the studio. So, you see, a fleeting glimpse of something is like eavesdropping. You don't know the whole story.

I know something. I have seen you, Bella. Have you forgotten what passed between us?

What? Nothing has passed between us.

At the party.

Bella looked at him and thought: I did not see him before. Her other painting was propped against the bottom of the easel, shielded from anyone's view but hers. She bent her head. It was far from finished, the outlines she held in her mind had not yet translated into much on canvas. Yet there was: dark hair, ice blue eyes, the shape of an arm.

The shock of realisation as visceral as the pain he'd caused.

Bella dipped her paintbrush in the jar of turpentine. She wiped her brush with an old rag and stored it with the rest of her paint kit.

This is over now.

Bella left the room.

28

Bella sat for a few moments, in a corner, and closed her eyes. When she tried to recall the image she needed, it would not come. She could see only faint copies, negatives. Or Randall, sitting before her, at ease.

Where could she go now?

29

Kate, I'm going to show you the portrait, and another painting. Neither is quite finished but I need your eyes.

That's rather thrilling. Has Randall seen his portrait yet?

No, you're the first.

You don't think he snuck a peek when you weren't looking?

If he has, he hasn't said anything.

Why don't portrait artists like their sitters to see a work in progress?

Because sitters rarely like what they see.

Yes, like when I look in the mirror first thing in the morning.

How we look on the inside never seems to match what we look like on the outside. If you think about it, we never see our true faces, not even in the mirror. By definition, we're actively looking at our face; we don't know how we appear when we're gazing off into the distance, or angry, or sobbing with sadness, or fear.

What about photographs?

They tell something of the story, of course. But in a mirror you're looking at yourself the wrong way around. You never see of yourself what others see, not exactly.

Do those details, those no one can see of themselves, reveal themselves to you?

Not always. You have to be prepared to look without expectation or prejudice. I tried very hard to do this with the second painting. It isn't my usual sort of work.

A different style?

It's partly that.

Tell me more.

There was a very specific reason why I wanted to do this painting. I wasn't sure if I was going to tell you, but I think I have to.

What was the reason?

This painting began as something else – a portrait without a sitter.

Of a real person?

Yes.

From memory?

Yes, in a way. A fractured memory. I thought if I did the portrait it would help me remember something I didn't want to remember but I hoped the act of painting would give me control over it.

I don't quite follow. The painting is of a person or something that happened?

A person, a man. Who had done something to me.

Who, darling? Done what?

I didn't know who it was, I never knew a name, never even saw him properly.

I see.

And without my knowing, it was connected to the other portrait.

What other portrait?

The one I've been doing here.

What, the portrait of Randall?

Yes. As you know, Randall is—

Complicated?

That's one word for it. When you asked me to paint Randall, I didn't think the two were one and the same but now I know they are.

Bella, this is all very odd. I can't say I follow what you mean. There's another person?

I thought there was, but there isn't. They're the same.

What is the memory you're recalling?

I'm getting to that. I can't do this easily.

Was it something horrible? I don't know that Randall should be mixed up in that.

No, that wasn't my intention at first. I thought painting Randall would help me understand him better, partly for you. But then, as I painted . . .

Tell me, Bella.

Something happened at that party, the first one I came to, at your house.

Well, I know that. I saw you, remember?

Not that, not quite. You gave me a blue pill, and I took it. I don't know what it was.

Just a little fun, darling. Harmless. A mood enhancer. You needed something to help you relax.

I've never done anything like that before. It made me feel so strange.

That's the point of it.

No, but, please, Kate. Listen to me, this is serious.
Let me say this. If I don't say it now, I'm not sure that I ever can.

You're frightening me now. What is it?

When I was dancing, I felt sick.

The pill wouldn't have done that. You must have drunk too much.

Perhaps. I was nervous when I arrived, and David had left me at the door, as he always does. I'm used to that but everyone seemed so glamorous, and confident. I didn't want to disappoint you, you see. I was afraid you would look across the room and see me being shy and pathetic, and that it would put you off, somehow. I wanted terribly for you to be pleased that I was there.

Of course I was pleased you were there. You don't have to put on a show for me, Bella-moo. You know I love you as you are.

Yes, but as you said yourself, I needed to relax. I was uptight. I knew that, too. Whatever it was, all I know is that I was feeling amazing and then everything started spinning, it was too much and—

Here, drink this. Just water.

Thank you. I'm sorry. I know I've got to tell you but I don't want to at the same time, and it's bringing it all back.

Come here, my darling, come here. Take it slowly; tell me when you're ready.

Sorry, Kate. I'm so sorry for what I'm about to say.

Shush. Whatever it is, I can take it. I'm a big girl, you know.

Randall took me upstairs, to the bathroom, so I could be sick.

That was kind. I didn't know he knew to be that kind.

He wasn't, Kate. He wasn't. I was sick, and he was still there. He was behind me, holding my hair, and then—

It's OK, it's OK. Catch your breath.

He left, you see. I thought I saw you.

I wasn't there, darling.

No. I don't know. Then there was someone else . . . I thought. But it wasn't it, it was—

Come here, Bella. Shush.

I can't, I can't tell you what happened. Look at the painting. You'll see it there.

30

Bella took the cloth off the portrait. It seemed suddenly naked without a frame, a rectangle of canvas propped on the easel. The paint was dry but there was still the strong smell of oils and turpentine coming off it. Her objective eye coolly appraised her own work. She knew she had caught the way in which the afternoon sun fell on the floorboards with a skill that demonstrated more than a knowledge of colour palettes. There was texture and detail in the chair, the rug beneath his feet, the book that was open on his lap. Most of all, she had captured his form perfectly. His body was long and lean, but there was a strength in his legs that could be glimpsed at from the way the material creased as they splayed open. One arm was thrown out, an unlit cigarette between his fingers, the other rested on his thigh, holding the pages. The posture was relaxed but there was no mistaking the gaze that stared directly out. His eyes were the blue of cold water, and she knew that he knew what he had done.

31

∞◇∞

He looks so unfeeling in it. Alex won't understand it, Bella. I don't know if I can give him this.

I can't change who he is, what he did.

He's Alex's son. He's Charlie's brother.

And?

I'm not prepared to martyr them to your cause, Bella. It's not even entirely clear what he did. You're not actually sure yourself, are you? Look, darling, I'm sorry you've had such a ghastly time, but it happens to us all, doesn't it?

What?

I saw the way the two of you were dancing together. He must have thought you wanted it.

You knew who it was all this time.

I didn't know what you say happened afterwards, did I? I only know what I saw. I knew nothing of what you're claiming has happened.

I think David left because of it. Has someone said something to him? Have you?

No, I haven't said anything but we know the minds of jealous husbands, don't we? We're all human. Randall's a young man, he must have just got overexcited. You didn't stop him?

No, I—

There you go, then. How could he know?

I wasn't in my right senses. That blue pill.

It's nothing to do with that. That was a little something that helps us relax. I use them all the time.

You're saying I should forget about it?

Yes. The number of times I've had to lie back and think of England ... You wait until it's over. I mean, there's no real harm done, is there? You're not pregnant?

No.

There you go. I think you have to put it down to a bit of mischief. I must say, I'm surprised at you, Bella. I didn't know you had such a devil in you, and there you were telling me not to do anything with John—

182

It's not the same. It's not the same thing, at all.

Oh, I think it is. I understand if it wasn't pleasant, and I'm sorry for that. He's difficult at times, I know.

More than that, even according to you and the things you have told me about the way he's behaved towards you.

Yes, but I probably don't make it easy for him, either.

How?

First of all, I'm the wicked stepmother, remember. And secondly, I am *me*, aren't I? I know you don't think I'm aware of it, but I am. I know I'm not everyone's tequila shot but that's fine with me. I like being difficult, swimming against the tide. You can't be like me and not expect to pick up a few enemies along the way.

No, but Kate, you can't excuse him, what he did to me—

I'm sorry for that, I am. But he's not so bad. He's a lost young man. And I'm too *much* for him. Too much woman, too much younger than his father. Too much not his mother.

Or he hates women.

You might be onto something there. It's not hard to understand why he finds us such a troublesome breed. I don't know if he's told you about his mother.

I can't forgive what he did. Don't ask me to do that. It's caused me—

Yes. The point is, Charlie adores him and Alex, though he tears his hair out over him, loves him and is very protective. He sees his faults as vulnerabilities. I'm afraid he was never any good at telling him off about anything. When Randall was ten, he poured a pot of decorator's paint all over Alex's car—

Why?

In protest against his father going away without him.

Didn't Alex punish him for it?

Apparently not. Guilt, you see, that his son had no mother.

Then perhaps the punishment needs to start now.

No, Bella. I think all you need to do is reframe the incident in your mind.

Incident?

Whatever it was. It was quick, it's over now, it won't happen again. Actually, I'm rather envious.

What?

You've been unfaithful to David. You've got your own back on him.

I haven't. It wasn't like that.

It was a bit, Bella. Why did you leave the
room with him?

I felt sick. I didn't know where the bathroom was.

Then why did you let him in the bathroom with you?

I was rushing to be sick, I didn't think—

That's what I mean. You weren't really thinking; you
went with your instinct. You didn't stop him, you let it
happen. One could argue you wanted it, on some level.

No, I—

No one would blame you. David might but there's
no need for him to know. It can be our secret. Has
Randall tried anything on with you again, since
that night?

No.

Has he mentioned it?

Possibly. I'm not sure. It was a veiled reference.

Are you sure it even happened? You said the pill made
you feel strange.

Well, I mean . . . I think so. It was all so quick and I
felt ill, I was on the floor of the bathroom. I think I
blacked out.

I think you should just put it away as a blip.

Yes.

Let's not think about it any more. But I do think you need to do something about the painting. Alex will mind terribly. He might be hurt after we've had you to stay.

I can't change it, Kate.

It's not who he is. It's not who he has to be.

It's who he is to me, it's who he is at this moment. I'm not saying he's without redemption, but you can't ask me to compromise my work.

Don't be so pretentious.

Pretentious?

Well, you are being, a tad. You're a good painter, but it doesn't make you Leonardo.

Nor do I pretend to be. As you said of yourself – I am me. This is who I am, and if it doesn't please you then so be it.

Very clever, flinging my own words back at me like that but you know perfectly well what I mean. Even the great masters had patrons, you know, commissions where they had to paint big noses smaller because of where the money was coming from.

Randall is not my patron.

No. But his father has shown you only kindness.

I'm not saying he hasn't. This has nothing to do with Alex.

It's his son, can't you see that? I can't have you hurt him.

For someone who has been hell bent on cheating on her husband lately, why are you being so protective all of a sudden?

Shush about that. And I'm always protective – I've never not loved him.

You've got a funny way of showing it.

It's different with John. We'll always feel this way, it happens whenever we see each other. It doesn't mean we don't love the people we're with.

That's handy for you, isn't it? Do you think Elaine will feel the same way?

She won't know. Nor will Alex.

You're lying to yourself if you think he's never going to find out.

People don't. Everyone likes to think they can always tell but they can't. You didn't find out about David, did you?

What? What do you know about David?

Only what anyone knows about him, Bella. It's obvious. To everyone but you, that is.

Why are you doing this to me?

I'm not doing anything to you, Bella. You're doing all this to yourself. This business with Randall, not confronting David.

OK. I can't do this any more.

Don't walk away from me. Bella. Stay. We need each other, don't you see that?

32

On the stove a pan bubbled gently with the warm and sticky aroma of raspberries turning to jam. Georgie stood on a chair, a little too tall for the arrangement, bending over the heat with a wooden spoon gripped by both her hands, stirring clockwise. Charlie sat at the kitchen table, watching her. Before him he had a plate with a slice of buttered bread, insistent on being the first to eat the finished goods, despite having been told that he would be waiting a very long time. Twelve empty jars stood on the table too, ready to be filled and given away. The children had made a list of people whom they deemed worthy recipients: their mothers, their fathers, the friendly woman in the village shop who let them have extra sweets, the man who fixed Charlie's bicycle.

Bella sat at the other end of the kitchen, a book open on her lap. She had read the last page three times without a word going in. Her role was kitchen monitor, though she had been warned by Georgie that she was not to interfere. She and Charlie wished to tell everyone that they had done *all* of the jam-making *by themselves*. Bella had readily conceded. She had been trying, and failing, to create a coherent plan to leave without going home. She couldn't talk to Kate; she didn't want to see David at the house.

Into this domestic scene came Kate, like cold wind through a barn door.

Georgie momentarily hesitated in her stirring, then carried on. Bella could hear the jam begin to boil. Charlie watched his mother more carefully but did not abandon his post, guarding the bread. Bella remained seated but folded her book and assumed a listening pose.

I've got an audition. It's tomorrow. I'll go up by train in the morning.

She came up closer to Bella, so she could talk more quietly. Her cheeks were flushed, her breath came in short gasps, as if she had been running up and down a flight of stairs.

What's it for?

A play. Not the lead part but close enough: the lead's best friend. Rehearsals start in three weeks, it would open at the start of December.

That's good timing. The children will be back at school by the time you start.

Yes, I suppose so. Bella, I think I've got a good chance of getting it. I worked with the director before, a while ago but we got on terribly well. I think he may have asked for me personally. And it's a proper production, in a decent theatre. A budget, in other words, which means costume fittings and props that aren't cadged from the stage manager's flat. I think we should toast to celebrate. There's a bottle of champagne in the fridge.

It's a little early.

We're celebrating the audition, not the job. I know better than that.

No, I mean, it's four o'clock in the afternoon.

Don't be such a stick in the mud. Tell you what, why don't you come with me? You could shop while I'm at the audition. Then we could have lunch together somewhere, before we train back.

David arrives tomorrow.

Yes, of course, so he does. Stupid of me to forget. Right, champagne. Don't say no, you're not as dull as that.

Kate opened the fridge and pulled out a bottle, then fetched two glasses from the cupboard. There was confidence and a flourish to her movements that Bella envied. Just as Kate started to twist the cork, Georgie called out that the jam was almost the right thickness. Charlie stood up suddenly, pushing his chair back with a noisy scrape on the floor. Bella started at the noise, and Kate must have done the same because in that same second the cork flew out of the bottle and hit Georgie's head. It was like a terrible domino effect that was unstoppable: too fast, too inevitable. Georgie stumbled on the chair, making it slip and as she fell she gripped the saucepan handle.

Bella did not know where the screams came from: her daughter, herself or a black abyss that belonged to the gods.

Blindly, she raced across the room and dragged Georgie to the sink, turning the cold tap on full. There was a mug by the side and she used this to throw water on to her child. The jam coated the front of her dress but had, miraculously, barely gone onto her face.

Georgie screamed and screamed.

Kate held Charlie, who was shouting loudly in distress.

Bella finally managed to cry out. *Get help!* It seemed as if Kate was moving deliberately slowly, and anger flooded into her fear, driven by the same adrenaline. Bella kept on throwing water on to her daughter's chest and stomach, still calling out, and then calling her daughter's name. So long as Georgie was screaming she was alive, she was breathing. But the pain belonged to them both.

When it seemed that the shock had started to ease a fraction, Bella found a pair of kitchen scissors and began to cut the cotton dress away. She peeled it slowly off her child's soft, scalded skin. The molten raspberries left a dark red stain that Bella could not look at. Cradling Georgie's head and shoulders in her lap, cooing and shushing her over and over, the sobs eventually began to subside, and their breathing became more even. When the ambulance arrived, Georgie had managed to drink a glass of water. The worst was over.

At least, that was what Bella thought.

33

Bella stayed in the hospital all night with Georgie, and in the morning her daughter was discharged. The scalding had been bad but with carefully applied dressings, it looked as if the blistering would not be as awful as first feared. In a few weeks, she should be healed. Physically.

Bella didn't telephone anyone, so they returned to the house by taxi. What she wanted to do was return home straight away but David was due to come down on the train that afternoon. Besides which, it wouldn't have been fair to move Georgie so soon. She was still tired and shaken from the experience.

The one relief Bella felt on returning was Kate's absence. She had departed for her audition, leaving the message that she would come back as soon as it was over. Bella wasn't sure she wanted to see her. There had been no apology so far for what had happened. Did she blame Kate? Yes, a little, if she was completely honest. She knew it wasn't fair, it was an accident, of course. But there was something about Kate's cavalier movements in all that she did, a carelessness towards those around her, that meant Bella couldn't help but accuse her of causing it. Why hadn't she been more careful in that kitchen, knowing Georgie was standing there with a pan of boiling jam?

Because she never saw anyone other than herself.

Bella put her daughter to bed, the curtains partially drawn, a jug of iced water beside her. Georgie was wearing a thin cotton nightdress over the gauze wrapped around her torso and did not want anything heavier than a sheet drawn up over her. Thankfully the room was warm, the sun shining outside. There would be people picnicking in that weather, or walking along a seafront eating ice cream. A frivolity that Bella couldn't imagine, like trying to remember how it felt to be cold when one was hot. She didn't resent them or blame them for it, she knew her own luck, too – it could have been so much worse than it was. But she was jealous of their care-free minds, a state of being that felt as distant to her as the innermost thoughts of a penguin.

Bella offered to read to Georgie but her daughter shook her head. She only wanted to lie and look out of the window, partially opened to let the faint breeze in. There was a tree close by, the occasional bird flying in to perch on a branch. Bella kissed her and said she would be back in an hour.

In her own room, as she had begun to think of it, Bella sat before the dressing table. She regarded her face and her hair. She knew that given what had happened she shouldn't care what she looked like when David arrived, but she did. She had not telephoned the house to tell him about the incident. There hadn't been time to think of it, and then at the hospital – when it became clear that it was bad but not life-threatening – she had decided that he did not need to know, not in the middle of the night. There was nothing he could have done, except come down a few hours earlier, and she hadn't wanted that. She didn't want to be diverted from caring for her daughter by dealing with David; she did not think he deserved to be forgiven simply because she hadn't the time or the inclination to be angry. What she needed to do right now was not to brush her hair but to get angry again.

Bella remained fixed in her seat, nothing but her own eyes looking back at her, and reminded herself of the fear and distress that David had put her through. If at any time she considered the possibility that his own fears had driven him away from her and Georgie, she immediately smothered the pity by recalling the desperation she felt when she telephoned nine different hospitals to ask them if he had been admitted. She remembered that half second before she opened a newspaper when she would pause, to brace herself in case she should see a photograph of his dead body as an unidentified murder victim. Like pricking herself repeatedly with a seamstress's pins, she recalled the abandonment and isolation that had been her only sensations as she lay in her bed night after night, knowing that whatever he was going through he considered it much more significant, more worthy of his attention, than anything he was putting his wife and daughter through. She allowed not one shred of sympathy.

It was a kind of meditation. It took her an hour and when she looked again at her face, there was colour and animation. Fury contorted her features, and her cheeks were pinched with the hue of it.

(She remembered the tiles on the bathroom floor, how their surface slipped like ice.)

She was ready to face him now.

34

Bella was with Georgie, sitting beside her daughter as she slept, whispering to her, when she heard them come through the front door. Her hand went to her own hair, then to her bare, dry lips. Carefully, slowly, she stood and left the room on tiptoe, closing the door gently behind her without a click. At the stairs she hesitated deliberately, listening for the movement in the hall. She felt unclothed, exposed to the slightest eddy in the air. The cool from outside had rushed in, disturbing the atmosphere, and she could hear Kate's shoes clacking on the floorboards, her half-shouts to Alex and Charlie. She could not hear David but she knew he was there. Kate's flurry of sound was intended to mute the shock that Kate knew Bella would feel, a warning signal of a kind to say: your husband is here.

Kate had known that David would be getting the two o'clock train; she must have made certain to find him at the station at the start of the journey. They must have talked. What would have been said? The possibility that she had been discussed made her feel dizzy.

Bella gripped the handrail and took the steps with what she knew was exaggerated stealth. They seemed very steep and she had the thought that if she fell, she could avoid the whole business of having to see him, greet him and be a grown up. She would prefer that he waken her with a kiss in a hundred years. And yet, she also longed to fly down those stairs, straight into his arms, and forget everything.

She tried so hard, she really did. But memories shoved themselves to the front of the queue, irate at being pushed back.

(The running of the tap water as she wet the flannel to clean herself.)

In the hall Bella saw the dumped cases, David's coat flung over them. Kate's bag was on the side, keys spilling out, a half-read paperback visible. As Bella tried to recall her prepared speech, her mind emptied like a drained bath. She couldn't remember if she meant to be angry or forgiving. Would she let him tell his side of the story? Did his side of the story matter?

Following the noise of the low chatter, Bella walked into the sitting room and almost crashed into Alex, who apologised, told her he was just coming to find her. Kate was standing by the window, Charlie beside her, his arms awkwardly wrapped around her hips, as if hoping she wouldn't notice. She had one hand on his head, as if to keep him still, while the other held a full glass. Her usual.

David was on the sofa, or rather, in the process of standing up as quickly as he could, his long legs awkwardly bending beneath him as he struggled to manoeuvre from the low seat, a tumbler of whisky in one hand. He looked ashen but she could see he had shaved and put on her favourite light blue shirt.

How is Georgie? Kate told me. Can I see her?

She's sleeping.

He nodded and came towards her, stumbled once. She remembered when they first met and he took her out dancing. He had been smooth lines and rhythms then, as if his feet could draw a perfectly scored piece of music on the floor-boards. The first time they moved together she had been exhilarated and amazed at how easily they stayed close. He made her feel as if she was the brilliant dancer and not as if he was leading her every step. Now, he moved his face towards her but she stepped back, as perfectly choreographed, only in reverse.

She took the advantage of her upper hand and regarded him in further detail. His cuffs were frayed, his shoes scuffed. She'd always liked his haphazard approach to dressing, his lack of regard for formality. Why now did her embarrassment sit uncomfortably in her chest? He was still handsome, still desirable, objectively speaking. Did she, Bella, desire him? She didn't know. Or didn't want to admit to it.

Alex went over to Kate and Charlie, touching his wife lightly on the shoulder and muttering something. Kate didn't look at him but sought out Bella's face, waiting for her authority instead. Bella nodded, and the three of them left without making any excuses or saying anything at all. In the room there was only her and her husband. He came towards her, too quickly for her to react, and pulled her into him, wrapped his arms around her and – she couldn't help it – her head bent down into that space she loved so much, the corner between his neck and his collarbone. She breathed in deeply and as she exhaled, her arms responded and found their way around him, her palms flat against his warm back. For a few seconds, she stayed like that, willing herself not to think or do, just be there.

It couldn't last.

When he spoke, it was soft and distinct.

I don't blame you for what happened.

What? Blame me for what?

Bella pulled her arms in, a cat drawing back her claws.

For Georgie's accident. I don't blame you.

I shouldn't think you would. It was an accident. It wasn't anyone's fault. If you want to point a finger, point it at Kate.

She felt disloyal. She'd lashed out in anger but caught the wrong person. He looked at her sadly.

I'm sorry, Bella.

Are you? Could you spell out for me exactly what you're sorry for? Because I'm not sure that's going to work. You're asking one small word to do an awful lot.

I think you need to say sorry, too.

I need to say sorry?

Yes. You took off, with my daughter, and I didn't know where either of you were. For days. I was out of my mind with worry.

Your daughter? Fuck's sake, David.

Fine, our daughter. You know what I meant. Why didn't you leave me a note?

I can't believe you're being serious about this. What about what you did to me?

I know my going off wasn't good, and I'm sorry for that. But I didn't take Georgie.

That doesn't make it all right, the fact that you went off by yourself to God knows where. Frankly, I took us both from the house because you needed to know what it felt like to be out of your mind with worry. I'm *glad* you went through that.

David finished his drink, and sat down heavily on the sofa. He put the glass down and ran his fingers through his hair, his head hanging. When he looked up again, the tiredness in his eyes made him look like an ancient god.

I know I'm not worthy but I love you. You're my wife, I want to make this better. Tell me what to do.

Bella's mouth was open but silent, her mind blank, when the door opened, jerking them both to turn around. Kate stood there, alone. She held out her hand and Bella took it, and they walked away together.

35

I don't understand, how did you get the train
down together?

You told me, remember? You said he'd be on the two
o'clock. And then I happened to be coming back at
that time, so I looked for him. I thought it would be
good, for you, I mean.

How?

I could prepare him.

Prepare him for what?

For what awaited him here. To apologise.

I thought you said if he came here it was because
then he would be on my territory. Why were you
helping him?

I wasn't, not like that. Bella, come on.

What did he say to you? On the train?

I'm sure he didn't say anything he wouldn't tell you.

I'm sure that he would. Please, Kate, tell me. I don't know what to think, I don't know what to do.

Did he mention the party to you?

No.

Do you think he saw me with—

We know he saw you dancing. I saw him watching you.

Oh God. I'm angry with him, for going. I am. But it's so exhausting to keep trying to hate him, when I don't. And I keep blaming myself, even while I tell myself that it's not my fault.

What isn't your fault?

All of it. Him seeing me with another man, what happened that night.

He shouldn't have gone without telling you.

I don't know what to do.

You don't have to do anything. He created this situation, remember. It's for him to solve, not you. Your job is to look after yourself and your daughter, nothing else.

Yes. You're right, I know. I don't want to make any decisions, though.

There's no need to make any decisions. You're here, and I'm looking after you.

Yes. I don't know what I'd have done without you.

You would have been absolutely fine, of course. But I'm glad you're still here. Aren't you going to ask me how my audition went?

Yes, sorry. How did it go?

Well, I think. You never really know with these things but I know the director, we chatted away easily enough. I had to do a quick read, which is always rather mortifying but I think I did OK.

When will they let you know?

Hopefully in a few days' time. Some of them are buggers, never tell you they've chosen someone else and you're left hanging on for weeks, clinging to the tiniest scrap of hope. But they said they would call my agent. Fingers crossed.

And toes.

Thank you, darling.

I'm sorry, I have to ask again. David – did he attempt to explain himself?

Sort of. That is, he started some sort of explanation but I felt I ought to tell him what had happened to Georgie.

Yes. You're right.

He reacted quite badly to that, understandably. I had to calm him down with a stiff drink. Luckily, I always have my trusty flask with me.

Do you?

No need to make that face.

Not making any face. Please. David . . . ?

Darling, is there anything he could have said to make what happened any better?

Probably not, but I don't see why that should stop him from trying.

I'm worried in case it makes it a whole lot worse.

What does that mean? Now I'm worried too.

You mustn't feel that you should have known, or even that there was anything that you could have done about it. I don't think you could have stopped him.

Apart from making sure we had a happy marriage?

Who can be sure of that? No one can do that alone. It takes two.

Don't start quoting to me out of a magazine.

I'm not, Bella. I know what you think of me and Alex—

Let's not get into all that now.

No, we won't. I think you must remember that he is only a man, and they are simple creatures, after all.

So you say.

I do say, and I know men. They can be very romantic and very sweet, but their heads are too easily turned.

Was David seeing someone? Has he been having an affair? How long has it been going on? What did he tell you, Kate? Tell me.

No, shush. He didn't say he was seeing anyone else. And I'm sure he wasn't. He loves you very much, that's clear for all to see.

What do you mean by their heads being too easily turned? Why did you say that just now?

Nothing, really. The only thing is, I think he saw me with John at the station.

You saw John?

Yes, we met for lunch after the audition. I didn't want to, honestly, Bella, but he was insistent, and I thought this time I could make it absolutely clear that nothing is going to happen.

Then something did.

Only a kiss. Bella, I can't help myself. It's like my body is taken over by a longing that has never existed before. It's exciting, and I need excitement.

Then why did you marry Alex?

Touché.

I'm sorry. I'm not trying to be rude. I'm curious. If you love excitement, if you need it, then why did you marry a man who is dependable and—

Boring?

I didn't say that.

No. He isn't boring, he's kind. I don't know why I married him. He was very persuasive at the time. I could ask the same of you. If you prefer to know where your husband is, why did you marry David?

I don't know. I thought I could change him, I suppose. The bits that weren't quite right, that is. There's plenty that I loved – still love – about him. But I don't want him to break my heart.

He won't. But I think you need to seduce him.

Seduce him?

Yes, win him back.

I don't understand what you're saying. It's crazy talk.

No, it's sane if you want to save your marriage. You want Georgie to grow up with her father.

I do want those things, but not if it means sacrificing myself. You haven't told me what happened when he saw you with John.

It wasn't anything. I shouldn't have mentioned it.

Well, you have. So tell me.

It's just that . . . in the first place, I don't know how he saw us. We were tucked away, not that far from the platform, I suppose. I don't know how long he'd been standing there when he saw us but when I realised he was there, immediately I could see that . . .

What? You could see what?

He was turned on.

I don't believe you. How could you tell, anyway?

Darling, please. I didn't say it to upset you.

And yet you did.

You mustn't feel badly about it. It happens to us all. Even after years we can discover extraordinary things about people we thought we knew.

That's certainly true. What were you doing with John?

We were kissing, no more than that. But it was—

I get the picture. You think David was turned on, watching you?

These things are contagious, aren't they? Alex worries whenever any of our friends divorce. He thinks it'll make me think of doing the same thing. Now your husband has seen me . . .

And it's going to make him think of being unfaithful? Or he thinks I've done the same?

I don't mean that exactly.

I need to get out. Stay here, in case Georgie wakes. I'm going for a walk.

When will you come back?

I don't know. I won't be long. But I can't talk to you any more about this.

Take a breather but you can't not talk to me, Bella. I'm the only one who understands you. The only one who knows who you are. We've been friends almost our whole lives. Who else can you say that about?

No, Kate, you're wrong. I'm alone. Whatever I need to do next, I'm on my own.

36

Bella walked around the garden three times before she went back inside. She needed to go to Georgie and now that her daughter was out of danger, she wondered if they could try to get a train home first thing in the morning. Of all the things she needed to know the only one she was certain of was that now he was here, she didn't want to be under the same roof as David after all.

The irony wasn't lost on her.

She headed for the kitchen, to fetch a new glass of water and some grapes for Georgie, to encourage her to eat something. But as she reached for the door, a noise from within stopped her. Two voices, male, low. One was David's, the other – Alex? Randall? She listened harder, checking over her shoulder to make sure no one was there to see her pressing her ear to the door.

The voices were increasing in volume but were then muffled by the sound of a tap running at full strength. When that turned off, she couldn't make out any consecutive words, only her and Kate's names. The tone of one voice was accusatory, the other defensive. A yell, and Bella leapt back from the door, a prescient instinct, as it flew open in the next moment and David marched out. He saw her and grabbed her by the wrist, taking him with her, before she could look into the kitchen to see with whom he had been arguing. Curiosity allowed her to be pulled by him, along the hall and up the stairs.

Where is your room?

Bella pulled her arm away from him.

I'm not taking you there now.

Yes, you are. We need to talk. I came here to see you, to talk to *you*, and everyone else is talking to me and it's fucking with my head.

I need to go and see Georgie; she'll be awake now.

No, she's still sleeping.

How do you know?

Kate took me, just now. I let her sleep, gave her a kiss.

I still want to go.

No. Not yet.

You don't have the right to tell me what to do.

In protest, like a small child, Bella sat down where she was standing, in the middle of the staircase. It seemed as good a place as any. She liked the transience of it. She was not committed to taking him to her room; she could at any moment leap up and make her way to Georgie. She didn't want to make a firm decision of any kind but to remain in limbo, halfway up the stairs, for the rest of her life. Let the rest of them go marching up and down.

Who were you talking to, in the kitchen?

Alex.

What about?

His marriage.

What about his marriage?

Not just his, ours too. He was telling me his *concerns*.

And he thought you would be someone to help? He went barking up the wrong—

He seems to think you and Kate are . . .

What? He thinks we're what?

In love with each other. It seems Randall saw the two of you kissing.

He didn't see that. But she's more of a lover to me than you are.

What does that mean?

Whatever you take it to mean. She would never take off without telling me where she was going or when she would be coming back.

I thought she did do exactly that?

Fuck off, David. Funnily enough, I don't feel that I have to explain myself to you right now. Not when you have yet to tell me where you went. Or why.

I left because I thought you would be better off without me, even if you didn't realise it at first.

You might have been right about that. But you don't get to make that decision by yourself, not when you're married and you have a child.

It wasn't a decision, I didn't calmly rationalise which was the best course of action. I left because I didn't know what else to do. It seemed the best way of protecting you and Georgie from me.

Where did you go?

Around.

Have you met someone else?

No, I haven't. But I gather you have.

What?

Stop this, Bella. You have no right to judge me after what you did. Alex confirmed what I saw at that party.

You saw nothing.

I didn't need to see any more. I know you. You're my wife. You forgot it in that moment. But I never forget.

What you think you saw, it wasn't—

It wasn't like that? Too easy. I didn't have you down as someone who would resort to such cheap clichés. And then, not only did you do that but you ran down here. You dare to accuse me of being unfaithful? After all this.

Fuck you, David.

If only you would. It's all I want. In spite of everything, I still want you.

In spite of *nothing*. I have done *nothing*.

Then nor have I. We're quits, shall we call it that?

No, we won't call it that, that's not what it is at all.

We could call it a marriage, but if you want to save it, we have to do something.

If I want to save it? I see, it's all down to me, is it? I broke it, so I must save it.

Yes. I'm here, aren't I? I've followed you, Bella. I'm here to bring you home, with Georgie, for us to try again.

I can't do that when you still haven't told me where you were, or what you were doing.

I don't see the point. There's no answer that will make you happy.

No answer you can give me will make me happy you mean, if it's to have a grain of truth in it.

I'm asking us to forgive each other.

There is nothing for which I need to be forgiven. And I don't know if I can forgive you, David – not yet.

When you are prepared to be honest with me, then perhaps we can talk.

All that you see here before you – is me. I can give you no more.

37

Bella lay beside Georgie, holding her daughter's hand, absorbing the warmth, stopping them both from falling. Georgie was still exhausted from her ordeal. Bella, too, felt bruised and tired. She could lie there, in the dark, for a few hours but she'd have to get up eventually.

Decisively, Bella went to her room and pulled out the suitcase. She packed what she had brought, then fetched Georgie's things and packed those, too. Outside it was dusk, the tips of the trees fluttering in the cooling evening air like a gentlewoman's wave. She had one more task, only that, and then she would take herself and her daughter home.

38

Bella went downstairs to the sitting room. The weather wasn't cold but the fire had been lit and she could see that the glasses and bottles for drinks had been set out. Kate came in, her freshly daubed scent clinging to her, her lipstick blood red, her hair shining. She was brisk, offering Bella a G&T, stoking the fire and then sitting on the sofa, waiting. Bella said nothing, sipped her drink, stared at the flames. She waited, too, though she didn't know for what. A sign, or prompt of some kind? She hoped she'd recognise it when it came.

After a few minutes, Alex came in, uncharacteristically in a clean shirt that had been put on for the evening, the smell of the starch strong. He muttered something to Kate and poured himself a whisky, no ice. The curtains had not been drawn and only blackness could be seen through the windows, as if a cloth had been thrown over the house, sealing them in. It had the same effect on them as on caged birds: no one spoke. Imagined lines of speech flashed through Bella's mind like Georgie's reading cards when she was five. But she could say none of them out loud, as if the syntax itself was too hard to enunciate.

David arrived, flustered but quiet, running his hands through his hair. He'd had a bath; Bella could see beads of sweat on his temple – he always took the water too hot. He nodded at Alex, accepted a glass of whisky, looked at Bella and sat down on the armchair that was too deep; he perched on the edge, his elbows on his knees. The absence of noise began to rush through Bella's ears but just as she thought she might have to break first, Randall came in.

Randall swept a glance over them with that particular mixture of bafflement and contempt the young reserve for the old. She did not look at him for long; she did not want to see his face, or for him to see hers. She was standing by the fire but now she moved closer to the mantelpiece, near enough to put a hand on it for support, should she need it. Randall got himself a drink and stood at the edge of their group, one hand jammed into his pocket.

Bella understood that the scenario had been planned, orchestrated and executed by Kate. Bella was the only one who had not been told to prepare for whatever game it was they were going to play. The only one who did not know the rules or how to win points. She had not bathed and dressed to kill. She felt the glass in her hand, heavy and full, and briefly wondered how much damage it would cause if she threw it. It was too solid to smash on anything but the hardest surface; it would not break on a skull. She took another sip.

What are you doing, Kate?

Kate, cross-legged on the sofa, drink almost finished, looked up at Bella, as if surprised.

I don't know what you mean. We're gathered here for a drink before supper in the normal way.

Kate gave a shrug, deliberately caught Alex's eye and gave him a complicit smile.

I see. In that case, as we're gathered here, perhaps everyone would like to see the painting?

David's head jerked towards Bella. She knew that questioning look but there were no answers he deserved.

I thought you said no one was to see it yet.

I changed my mind.

As you know, I've seen it.

Why don't you tell everyone what you thought?

Careful, Bella.

I'd like to hear it, Kate, what you make of it. I think we'd all like to hear it.

The men in the room saying nothing, the volley of words between the women only. Well, so what? Each one of them had presumed power over her or Kate at one point or another. They could wait this time. Bella's strength was surging through her, unlocked from a door to which she hadn't realised, until now, she held the key.

On Kate's face, bewilderment. Her sure footing had given way beneath her, and it was a novel sensation. When she spoke, it was soft.

Darling, let's not do this now, not like this.

Randall shifted on his feet, watching them both.

Is this the painting of me you're talking about? Is it finished? Can I see it?

David stood up and walked over to Bella. He didn't touch her but she felt his breath on her face.

I don't know what you're doing but stop it. Now.

Bella laughed. Fear, fury and exhaustion had brought her to this point. But also love. It was there, if mostly in disguise. It came from her and attached itself to people and seemed to do so without guidance or instruction. She loved her daughter, not because she had to, not just because she was her mother but because she thought Georgie was pretty wonderful. She was a good, sweet girl. That love made sense. What was that same love doing attaching itself to David, to Kate? It was a love with no sense, that turned in on itself, revolted, went black and strangled her. It did her no good.
Enough.

I'm not doing what you tell me to do. Never again, David.

Kate stepped forward.

Darling—

No, nor you. You have controlled and manipulated
your husband, your stepson and my husband against
me, and I didn't see it before but I see it now. I saw
it in my painting. Randall hardly knows what he
did to me—

Randall held his hands up, as if starting to protest,
but stopped.

But he did do it. It was not of my doing.

Alex, always so quiet, as unobtrusive as a wristwatch,
cried out.

What are you doing? What are you saying about my
son? What did he do?

I will not tell you that. Ask him, not me. Go and see
the painting, you will find the answer there if you
know how to look.

Is this something you and Kate have done together?
Some plot, against us? Women versus men?

Alex, floundering in these unfamiliar waters.

No.

Bella turned to Kate.

One last chance. Will you defend me, or not?

Kate looked at Bella.

Don't ask that of me.

Then . . .

Bella put her glass down, carefully, on the mantelpiece.

. . . I'll ask nothing of you again.

39

For a split second, everything was completely still. A cry from upstairs was heard and then, one by one, like marbles on a slope, they spilled out. Bella first, David following, then Kate, Randall, Alex. In the hall their running footsteps echoed and no one spoke. His wife already out of sight, David went up the stairs, his hand on the bannister, pulling his long body up, his lungs heaving. Kate kicked off her shoes in the hall, her feet soft on the tiles, leaving dark smudges of sweat. Randall close behind, Kate's shadow on him, his face set. Alex, last of all, limbs awkward from confusion and fear. The three of them went into the studio.

The easel was standing in the middle of the room, the legs of the wooden structure splayed like a man's, but where the folded arms should have been was the canvas. Propped up on the floor was the second painting, unfinished, the places where the memory had failed still blank. It was abstract, if you wanted to call it something, the dark colours thickly daubed to create textures and disturbed lines. Perhaps the trace of two figures, a hand on another's waist. A doorframe. A thin trail of crimson.

The painting that stood before them, eye to eye, was unequivocally of Randall. He regarded himself with coolness on either side.

Kate went to knock the painting off but Alex held her arm. He asked his wife to explain what was going on, for once and for all.

In the police statement both Alex and Kate said separately, unanimously, that the rifle should never have been in that room. Neither of them knew for certain who could have left it, laid across the arms of the chair where Randall had sat for his portrait. They assured the police that there was a safe for the gun, with a lock, and the key was kept in Kate's room, in a matchbox covered with seeded pearls. No thief, they said, could find it there.

40

Bella and Georgie, in a taxi, around the corner on their way to the station, going home. Georgie, half lying on her mother's lap, buried her head inside Bella's coat and held onto her tightly, saying nothing. If they didn't hear it, if they couldn't see it, perhaps it didn't happen.

SEVENTY-SEVEN

1

Bella was working in her studio when the telephone rang. She stared at the handset for a moment or two, willing it to stop. She knew there was no one else around to answer it yet she couldn't help but wait to hear Harry call out that he would get it, not to worry. With a small breath of frustration she put her paintbrush down and stood, careful not to make another noise as she did so. Georgie had reminded her often enough that only old people made a sound every time they sat down or got up. She couldn't prevent a grimace through her tightened lips: her lower back was stiff after the hour or so she had spent perched on the stool, deep in concentration. She was trying out a new style of painting and was hopeful it might work though it was too early to tell yet. If it did, she might keep her gallery's interest for another year.

The telephone was still ringing. That meant either a man selling kitchens or her daughter. She knew which she would prefer, then told herself off. She loved to talk to Georgie but wished her only child would remember that she needed to work when the sun was up. Young people seemed to think that Bella's generation had nothing to do but lie around waiting to hear from them.

She walked across the room, only a few steps, and picked up the phone. Her eyes fell on the messy pile of bills, letters and old Christmas cards stacked beside it, weighted down by a stone that had been painted by Georgie's boy, her only grandchild, a few years ago. She would sort them out today. It wasn't the first time she'd said it to herself, but today she meant it. And she didn't say it out loud – she hadn't got to that point, not yet.

Bella adjusted the waistband of her trousers as she held the phone to her ear. Wretched things, shrinking in the wash.

Hello?

Good afternoon, may I speak to Mrs Conville?

No, you mayn't. Not any more, I mean. I'm Mrs Larkin now. Who is this?

I do apologise, Mrs Larkin. You don't know me but my name is Roger Turnbull. I'm ringing on behalf of Mrs Katherine Clifford, though she has said you will better remember her as Kate.

Kate?

Yes, does that name mean anything to you?

Bella's grip tightened on the handset. She looked outside but nothing had changed; the rain was still in the distance.

Has something happened to her? I've not heard from Kate for . . . well, I don't know. Is she dead?

No, she's very much alive. It's been thirty-five years since you last saw each other, she says.

Who are you, exactly?

Mrs Clifford is one of my clients, I run a long-term care facility.

An old people's home?

Some call them by that name, yes. We prefer long-term care facility.

And Kate is one of your clients?

Yes.

I see.

I know this must seem rather an intrusion but Mrs Clifford has been very keen to speak to you, and we tracked you down—

I'm not prey, I hope, Mr Turnbull.

Ah, no, no, of course not. Apologies. Bad turn of phrase. In fact, it wasn't very hard to find you once Mrs Clifford remembered you were an artist. You have quite a considerable reputation, Mrs Conville, I mean Larkin. Sorry.

Yes, I got my success under my old married name. I suppose a gallery gave you my number?

The Simon Phillips Gallery.

Must be more than fifteen years since I exhibited
there but we would have sent them a change of address
card. That's all beside the point. What does Kate want
with me now?

She'd like to see you, if possible, or talk to you on the
telephone.

Is she with you now?

No, I thought it best to talk to you privately first.

Yes, you were right to do that. I'm going to have to
think about it. Is she unwell?

Physically, she is in reasonably good condition.

For her age, you mean?

If you'll forgive the expression.

It's all for our age these days. The problem is
in the mind?

It's hard to say. I can't repeat anything that is
confidential patient information, you understand. But
we believe it would do her a great deal of good to see an
old friend.

I'm not sure I fit that description.

I beg your pardon?

I am not yet old, though I know some would call
me that. And I haven't been Kate's friend since I

last saw her. Or rather, the last time I saw her we were decidedly not friends. I'm not inclined to come running just because she's snapped her fingers after three decades of silence.

I understand, Mrs Larkin. Perhaps you might permit me to leave you with our telephone number, in case you change your mind?

No, I don't think so, Mr Turnbull. There's no message. Goodbye.

Bella put the telephone down before she could think any further. She saw her hand was trembling, and she wondered if perhaps she should have asked a question or two. But she gave a shake of her head, as if to toss the thoughts out, and went back to her stool. She put the radio on, someone playing the piano, and went back to her work. She would try to give Georgie a call later. It had been a few days since they had spoken, and perhaps they could start to make a plan for a weekend together. Bella fancied cooking a leg of lamb very slowly, slashed and slathered in butter and herbs, with a couple of bottles of the good Rioja that Harry had loved so much.

With that, any thoughts of Kate were firmly dismissed.

2

∞

Why do you think she's in an old people's home? She can't be old enough. Aren't you the same age?

Yes, we are. I don't know. I didn't ask.

Aren't you curious?

No, not really.

I don't believe you, Mum. I can remember her very well, you know.

Can you? It was such a long time ago.

Yes – what was I? Nine or ten, I think. But everything lasts longer when you're a child, doesn't it? The summers seem twice as long as they do now, so they stick in the mind. I remember that house. Why did we go there in the first place?

Oh, Georgie, I don't know that I'm in the mood for this.

I am. I never ask you about that time, I know you don't like looking back—

I really don't.

But it's my history, too. I want to know. One day you'll be gone—

Thank you for the reminder.

You know what I mean. You'll be gone and then I won't be able to ask you questions any more.

Hallelujah.

I'm going to ignore that. Go on, we've got a bit of time for once. Here, have another glass of wine. And tell me why we went down there.

Your father had disappeared, I didn't know where. It was only for a few days at first but Kate and I had resumed our childhood friendship not long before. We didn't need much excuse to spend some time together and she suggested that I go down to her father-in-law's place, with you, so that we wouldn't be there when your father eventually decided to come home.

That's cold.

Maybe. But I was so angry, and it was driving me spare to be in the house either worrying or raging. It wouldn't have been much fun for you. Other things were going on, too.

What other things?

Nothing I want to go into now but I needed distraction. Kate was offering to look after me, and I think it had been so long since anyone had done that. I'd been on my own since Granny died.

You were married to Dad.

Yes, but husbands didn't really look after their wives, in that sense. Or mine didn't. I was very in love with your father but he was exhausting.

He did used to look after me, though.

Yes, he did, when he wasn't working. He loved you so much.

Even if he buggered off.

It was nothing to do with you.

Mum, I'm forty-four now, you don't need to keep reassuring me.

I know, darling. You're still my little girl, you see.

Yes, I know. Go on, tell me more about when we went to Kate's.

I thought this was a trip down your memory lane, not mine. It was a complicated time for me, I'm not sure that I want to remember it.

Remember Kate, then. Just generally – I still don't understand how you could have fallen out so completely, not when you were such old friends.

We'd fallen out before, when we were seventeen. Some people never change. That's why I don't want to see her now.

But she's the only person who knew you as a little girl, who knew your granny.

At my age, hardly anyone remembers me as a little girl, least of all me. You won't understand it yet but when I look back on that early part of my life, it's as if it happened to someone else. It almost did happen to someone else, one changes so much.

How have you changed?

I think I was rather shy then. I was easily intimidated, and Kate intimidated me. Paradoxically, she brought me out of myself, I'll give her that. She gave me a confidence I didn't think I'd ever have. But she was capable of ripping it away with a word. After that last time, I realised I was better off without her.

And without Dad.

Yes, having the courage to throw her off also gave me the courage to end my marriage. I know that was hard on you but we had fun together, didn't we?

We did.

Do you think your father found happiness in the end?

Perhaps. He never has any money, that makes it harder.

I gave him money until you were eighteen.

Did you? He never told me that.

No, he wouldn't. It would have embarrassed him.
That's me done, darling. I'm off to bed.

You won't get in touch with Kate, then? Not at all?

Why are you so eager for me to do that?

Because you don't seem to have many friends around.
And I can't see you as often as we'd like. I'd be
comforted to know you have the company of an old
pal, that's all.

Just because she's old doesn't mean she's to be trusted.
That's my last word on the matter. Goodnight
Georgie, sweet dreams. Sleep tight—

Mind the bed bugs don't bite. I will, Mum. Love you.

Love you too.

3

Bella recognised the writing on the envelope. She still used brown ink, and though the letters were rather shakily set down, the sloping angle was the same as it had been when Kate was fourteen.

Bella put it on the pile, under the painted stone.

Not today.

Not tomorrow, either.

4

Jenny died. It was swift, for that they had to be grateful, if nothing else. She'd had the news the week before that her cancer had come back, everywhere, and she wasn't going to have long. Alone in the house, she must have tripped at the top of the stairs, no one knows how, but by the bottom step she lay, her neck broken. Her husband was distraught, as were her children: they hadn't had a chance to say goodbye.

Bella had become one of Jenny's greatest friends, seeing each other at least once a week even when their children were no longer at school together. They talked on the telephone and holidayed together as a foursome, when Bella married Harry. Jenny had been kind to Bella, always, as she was to everyone. A good listener but funny, too. When Bella sat down in Jenny's kitchen the anticipation of the laughter and honesty that was about to come would arrive as a physical sensation in her throat. It almost choked her with the things she wanted to say to Jenny that she couldn't say to anyone else. They had been friends for over thirty-five years, and Bella was asked to give a reading at her funeral. Afterwards, at the wake, Bella talked dutifully to Jenny's other friends and wider family, as the unofficial bridge between their mutual dead friend and Jenny's husband and children. Yes, Bella nodded, over and over again, it was so sudden, so sad, who knows how Robert will cope, thank goodness for the children, Jenny was such a wonderful wife and mother, we'll all miss her terribly. Hardly anyone knew the cancer had come back and those closest to her decided to keep it a secret, as they didn't want anyone to think she had fallen down the stairs deliberately.

Back home, Bella marched on. She painted in her studio, she telephoned her gallery and said she would manage three more paintings by the end of the year, and she started carefully to plan her Christmas presents. There was an ache in her chest that thudded when she accidentally reached out to pick up the telephone but it wasn't so sharp or painful as when Harry had died, and she felt that though it was sad, it was, somehow, manageable and even sometimes beautiful. Her friendship with Jenny had meant something and it was only right that she should miss her and feel bereaved.

All of that was fine. What was not fine was opening a cupboard to take a cup out and there being something in the flash of sunlight on the china to prompt a memory that, moments later, had her in a flood of tears. There was no mistaking the hollowness in her stomach and a true, deep yearning to be with Kate.

This, unleashed, like a wild cat that prowled around her mind, led to nightly dreams in which Kate accused her of abandonment. Kate would appear as a young woman, her dark hair thick and wavy, her eyes fixed on Bella, asking her where she was, how could she leave her and all they both needed was each other. Then she would take Bella's hand and the two of them would start to run, over fields and through woods, branches scratching at their bodies, until Bella woke, sweat pouring between her breasts.

Fiercely Bella would mutter to herself as she walked around the garden, deadheading the last of the autumnal flowers. She pulled the petals off, reciting an inversion of the 'he loves me' incantation, to rid herself of this intrusive, unwelcome desire to look up Mr Turnbull's telephone number. She tried to work but could not concentrate, and she was tired to the marrow after her sleepless nights. The last time she had felt this bone-aching exhaustion had been when she was pregnant with Georgie. In the middle of a supper party with David, she would drop out of the conversation and indulge in long and detailed fantasies about getting into a bed with milk-white, crisp linen sheets and falling into a dreamless sleep for days. She'd forgotten that, till now.

So many memories had started to press in, unprompted, uninvited. She could feel the seams of her carefully ordered and controlled life coming apart, the stitching getting looser. Bella reminded herself more than once to think of Harry, not David. In the act of trying to remember what to put on her shopping list, David would flash into her mind, the picture of him bending into the fridge, asking her where the butter was. Her fingers trembled as she unknotted her shoelaces while Kate's voice echoed, telling her that men liked heels on a woman and who couldn't be sympathetic to the Victorian lust for ankles?

Georgie was right, she didn't like to look back, had never been that sort of person. Bella preferred to face ahead with a heart full of optimism and strength. Unlike many of her whining contemporaries and their complaints about loud

240

noises and losing their specs, Bella liked the company of young people, to hear about the new and strange world they inhabited. She listened to their music and watched their films, amused by the language she didn't understand. It was as it should be: Bella believed she had had her time and now it was for the younger ones to take things on. She wished to paint, to exhibit and to be busy, but she had no inclination to indulge ambition. Without Harry at her side – he had always urged her on, had such a gusto for trying new things – she hoped only for a quiet, constructive existence, watching the world as a thoroughly entertained member of the audience. The very last thing she wanted was Kate, who would transport Bella back to the person she was half a lifetime ago and beyond. It would make her self-conscious, unveil those tiny, otherwise insignificant choices she made about the way she lived her life, dressed and decorated her house. No one else cared – no one alive, that is.

Kate might.

5

In the dead of night, the thin layers of memories unpeeled themselves and floated into corners of Bella's mind that she had thought long since locked away.

Cold tiles.

Blue eyes.

A matchbox covered in seed pearls.

'Tragic Death of a Young Man' on page seven of the newspaper.

Bella closed her eyes and tucked her head into her folded knees but it was no good: the images remained as clear as dew on the early-morning grass.

6

Unlocked, unleashed, Bella suffered weeks of days and nights lived at half-mast; a greyness that seeped into her sight and movements, grinding her to a near halt, and yet somehow a will to go on remained.

Then, for four nights in a row, Bella did not sleep at all.

On the fifth morning she inched her way down the stairs to the kitchen, pain shooting from her knees to her hips on every step. She went to put the washing on but there was none in the basket: she had worn the same clothes all week, even her knickers. In the fridge was half a brown apple, smoked mackerel with white spots showing on it and three soft carrots. She had run out of milk and butter.

First, she telephoned the doctor for sleeping pills and arranged to collect them in the afternoon, reassuring the young physician that she wouldn't take them too often. She had done this only twice before, in the months after Harry died, when Georgie insisted she get them, but Bella had shied from using even one, frightened of becoming dependent on them. So now she would have three full boxes. It should be enough.

The decision made, energy surged through her, like a second wind at a party an hour after you'd wanted to go home. She found a box of crackers that weren't too stale and crunched on them for her breakfast. She wasn't hungry but if her stomach was too empty, the vodka might go straight through. Holding onto the rush, she had a bath and put on clean underwear and an ironed shirt with a skirt that she'd worn at Harry's last birthday, not that they had known at the time that it was his last. As she dressed, she pictured her skeleton inside herself, an anatomical study in monochrome; she was sure she could feel each bone and tendon. Dispassionately she pinched the skin on the back of her hand and watched it slowly go flat again. Bella had long fallen out of the habit of looking in the mirror and never with her glasses on but she stood before it today and peered at herself with wry amusement – was she blonde or was it cheating if her hair was white? Her eyes were blue, not fading in the least, and her figure was passably OK. She had to concede that she wouldn't have been happy with it at twenty-seven but she was at seventy-seven. It just didn't seem to belong to her.

Bella rinsed out her bath and basin, put bleach in the loo and cleaned out her tooth mug, grimacing at the inch of yellow gunge that was at the bottom of it. She put her towels and bath mat in the laundry basket, then made her bed with clean sheets. This was quite exhausting and after she had smoothed the top blanket she sat on the low chair by the window to catch her breath. Two pigeons were sitting side by side on a telephone wire that was close to her house. They pecked at each other's feathers and side-stepped to and fro, flirting, or so she liked to imagine. People were always so dismissive of pigeons and it was true they were bullies at the bird table with loud coos that drowned out the more delicate notes of the woodlark. But Bella liked the way they chatted to each other and the dramatic flap, like flags in the wind, when they flew onto her lawn. Bella took her time watching the birds and thinking about these things, enjoying herself tremendously. It had been a long while since she had done this.

Back down the stairs, less painfully this time, and Bella went into her studio. There were several mugs, some of which were full with cold tea, and she cleared these into one corner, emptying them out into the plant pot. The long dark green leaves had tapered to crispy brown fronds but it was alive and would drink. She edged it closer to the French doors, where it would get more light. Georgie would probably chuck it out but it may as well get what it could. The painting Bella was working on, a square canvas with a bird so simply portrayed it might have been a linocut print, she left propped on the easel. She hadn't painted a portrait since – well, she wouldn't think about that now. The finished paintings were stacked neatly at the side and there were several sketches in the drawers of her plan chest. Her paints were always well organised, kept in the correct colour order, her brushes cleaned at the end of each working day. The walls had been painted plain white a long time ago but were covered with various postcards and drawings she had accumulated, tacked up with pins and sometimes on ribbons. They formed a sort of wallpaper collage and each one could take her down a new trail of ideas, which was why they were there. She had never needed memories and did not like them forcing themselves upon her, making her cry when she bit into a crisp apple or heard a song on the radio.

She looked at the telephone and narrowed her eyes. The pile of letters and papers beside it was threatening to become too unwieldy even for the heavy stone to keep it all in place. The stone was the first – the only – thing to give her pause, with its gaudy swirls of acrylic paint her grandson had painted with such enthusiasm when he was three. She loved him very much and did not like to think of how her death would be explained to him. His mother would find the right thing to say – she was good at that.

She knew she ought to telephone Georgie but it might make her daughter feel much worse – if she looked back and thought she could have said something to change her mother's mind. Georgie would be sad, of course, but the day would have had to come sooner or later so why not now? Swiftly, when she was in her right mind and not ebbing away into nothing. She couldn't stand the thought of that, not being able to do anything for herself, and a burden on Georgie, too. And she couldn't live any more with the thoughts that haunted her.

Standing in the doorway of her room, the only sound a faint call of the pigeons, she watched the dust motes swirl in the yellow sun. All that remained was to get in the car to collect her pills, come home and get into bed.

7

Everything was very bright, the light pulsing on her eyelids. Without moving, she attempted to feel whether or not her body existed. She had the terrible sensation that it did.

There was a quiet murmur of voices, one male, one female. She was lying on her back and wanted to turn but could not instruct the right muscles to make it happen. She tried to listen to what they were saying but the sounds faded in and out. Who were they and why were they talking? She knew without opening her eyes – even if she could – that she was not at home but she had no idea where she was instead. She had no memory of leaving her house. She tried to remember a basic fact about herself but could not. Names floated to the surface but none of them seemed to fit. Was she nine years old, or twenty-two or a hundred? Her stomach was hollow but she had no hunger; her throat was sore but she had no thirst.

Whatever it was anyone wanted her to do, they would have to decide on it for her. She could not think any more. She slept, and the only thought that made sense was the one about a handsome prince – or were there two? – coming to kiss her awake. She hoped he came soon.

8

When Bella opened her eyes, Georgie was sitting beside the bed. This was a surprise. She couldn't remember any plan for Georgie to come for a visit, and she didn't usually arrive before Bella was awake. Bella generally got up quite early these days, not needing so much sleep now she was older—

Fuck.

Shame lay on her body with its oppressively heavy weight. She tried to close her eyes tight but it was too late. Georgie had seen her.

Mum? Mum, are you awake? Are you there? Can you talk to me? Are you OK? What can you see?

Georgie broke down into sobs, and then another voice, a woman, was saying calmly not to overexcite her mother.

Sorry, I'm sorry.

She'd failed. How could she have failed? She'd taken so many pills and drunk the vodka. She didn't want to be awake, to face her daughter. Georgie would blame herself, would think she hadn't been listening hard enough or something and it was nothing to do with any of that. She had had enough of loneliness, that was all. She wanted David.

No, not David. Not him. Who was it?

Harry. She wanted Harry. Perhaps. Someone, anyway. Jenny? Not even Jenny.

No one. She didn't want anyone at all. Couldn't they all fuck off out of this room and leave her to it? Why did they save her? She didn't want this life any more, she'd lived it for seventy-seven years and that was enough. All that lay ahead was decline and falls, broken hips and struggles, memory loss and no appetite. She'd heard people say that they didn't even enjoy drinking wine any more. Oh, fucking sod all that.

But then, Georgie, crying. That hurt more.

Bella opened her eyes again.

I'm so sorry, my darling. I didn't mean to do it.

Georgie snapped her head around, wiping the tears off her face, trying to give a wide smile, telling her mother not to be sorry, things would be better now, she wouldn't leave her alone any more.

Oh, Christ no. If she was going to have to stay alive she wasn't leaving her house. She didn't want to sit in the corner of her daughter's kitchen, a thousand miles away from anyone or anything she knew, listening to the family shout, the doors slamming and everyone talking about things that were so incomprehensible they seemed to be conversing in another language.

She needed to talk to Georgie about this but she couldn't. She was too tired. The important thing was to wake up and stop them all from making decisions about her life, keeping her alive, without consulting her. Everyone treated old people like children and they'd be feeding her with spoons quicker than she could say 'get out' if she didn't take control of this soon.

In a minute, though.

Just a little more sleep first.

9

The next time Bella woke she was alone. She lay there for some minutes, staring at the white ceiling and the light fitting, which seemed rather precariously nailed in. It was directly above her and if it should choose that moment to snap – it looked as if it could – it would smash upon her head. It wouldn't kill her, worse luck, but it would be very painful. How long would she have to lie there with a broken light fitting on her head before anyone noticed? Perhaps then she would bleed to death but it would be very slow and painful, she didn't like the idea of that at all. She might as well live.

She was in a hospital, she could see that much. In a room by herself, for which she gave thanks. The bed was iron, painted white like every other immovable object in there. The sheets had a stiffness that came from overboiling rather than starch. A clipboard was hanging from the rail at her feet but she couldn't see what was written on it. On the bedside table was a vase of drooping flowers. Whoever had put them in there hadn't given them enough water, and it was hot in the room too. The small window was sealed shut. She could hear people walking past in the hall outside, the metallic clang of trolley wheels and a faint, acrid smell of vegetables, presumably cooked in the same way as the sheets. Bella put her hands by her sides and pushed herself upright, as she always did, as she always would.

10

Georgie took Bella home. The house stood silent and dark, reproachful of Bella's attempt to abandon it. Bella dreaded the shame that would wrap itself around her as soon as she stepped in through the front door but Georgie went a few paces ahead, switching on lights and talking in a singsong way about the things she had done to make coming home nicer. She had cleaned the fridge, washed the floors, dusted the bookshelves and bought fresh flowers. Bella bit her lip.

There was a chicken in a bag of shopping Georgie had brought, and soon they had it roasting in the oven. The smell of it cooking, and the simple act of setting out the cutlery and napkins helped a little. Bella sat down while Georgie peeled and chopped carrots, washed the greens and busied herself around the kitchen. Bella was both grateful and longing to be alone. She supposed anything that remained of the pills would have been cleared away, and so had all the alcohol, judging from the empty wine rack. Georgie didn't need to be afraid, but Bella couldn't bring herself to say that out loud.

Supper on the table, a candle lit, Bella and her daughter sat opposite each other.

Bella looked at her plate with the steam rising from the vegetables, the skilfully carved chicken, the thick gravy. Her appetite disappeared completely as she picked up her knife and fork. She knew the food would have the texture and taste of mulched cardboard as soon as it went in her mouth.

Mum, I need to talk to you.

Do you, darling? I don't know that I'm yet quite up to discussing—

No, not that. Don't worry, we'll talk about that another time when you – if you – want to, or I can arrange for you to see someone. Professional, I mean.

If you think that's a good idea.

I do. But we need to talk about your living arrangements.

Yes, I suppose we do.

Mum, I'm really sorry but I don't think you can come and live with us. The house is too small and it's too far away from anyone you know, and I know I said it at first but we've been talking it over and—

My sweet girl. It's very kind of you to have even thought of it in the first place but I'm perfectly fine in my own house, I don't want to live anywhere else. I'm too old to move now, everything is here.

Yes, I understand that. I thought that, too, although I worried I was trying to make myself feel better about you not coming to live with us. But I don't think you should be by yourself.

Oh, people are always telling me to get a dog but I don't want one and I'm getting older now, it'll be too much to take it out for walks soon. Besides, one can't go off anywhere. Dogs are more trouble than babies, you know, less portable.

No, I don't mean a dog.

I could get a cat, I suppose?

You could, a cat would be lovely, but that wasn't what I was talking about, either. I'm talking about a person, a friend. Someone to keep you company, someone to talk to and do things with.

Georgie, I don't want anyone else living here. And even if I did, none of my friends want to come and live with me, they all have lives of their own. Husbands, children – dogs, even.

That's it, you see, there is one friend who wants to come. Is coming, in fact.

Is coming?

Yes, I knew you would fight me on this but, Mum, I know it's the right thing to do, so I've gone ahead and told her to come, and she's arriving tomorrow. Before I leave, so I can help settle her in—

No, wait. I don't want anyone living here. I don't know anyone who could. Who is it?

You can't be on your own.

Yes, I can. I'm a grown woman. I'm your mother, don't forget.

I don't forget. But I'm going to insist on this.

Who is it?

Kate.

Kate?

Yes. I was clearing up in your studio and there was a whole pile of letters by the telephone that you hadn't opened—

Did you open them?

Yes, Mum, I did. I was worried in case there were unpaid bills – I've paid your telephone, by the way – and there were letters from a man who said he had spoken to you, he runs a long-term care facility—

You had no right to open my post.

I did when you had—

Fine. I'm cross about it but I'm not going to talk about that now. Why is Kate coming here? I don't want her to come. I haven't seen her or spoken to her in decades, and there's a reason for that, you know. I know you were young when it happened, but you can't have forgotten.

I haven't forgotten. I know it was all very upsetting at the time but, as you say, it was a long time ago.

Why do people think the passing of time makes everything better? It doesn't. Slavery was a long time ago – does that mean we should bring it back?

Mum. This is different, you know it is. I think you both need each other, could help each other. Kate wrote, too. She has no money, she can't pay the bills at the home, she has to leave—

What about her husband? Why can't he look after her? Oh, Georgie, you don't know what you've done.

I don't know but something must have happened to him. The point is that she's – well, she's desperate. And so are you.

I'm not.

Really? Because that's not how it looked when—

Yes, all right. I know that was a low point but I've realised my mistake, and it's not going to happen again. It was just a moment of madness.

That's it – I don't think it was. I think you've been depressed for a while. Look at your work.

What about my work?

We don't need to go into that now.

Yes, we do. What do you mean, look at my work?

You've been working on the same painting for most of this year.

That's because I'm trying out something new, a different technique. I think the gallery will be pleased to see it.

Hmm.

When did you become an art critic?

We're going off the point. I don't want to talk about your work. I'm only saying that since Harry died, and then Jenny, I think you've been lonely. It's made you depressed. There's medication but that's not the only treatment—

It's nothing that millions like me don't have to contend with. And I'm one of the lucky ones, I have work – whatever you think of it – and I have my own house.

Yes, I know all that but you don't have to contend with it. You could find new purpose.

In *Kate*?

Yes, in Kate.

She's not, in case you've forgotten, the most supportive of people.

I know she could be tricky, but I think she's changed in old age. I've spoken to her. She's excited about seeing you. Look, if it doesn't work we'll sort something else out—

How? You've put me in an invidious position. I'd have to evict her. It's insane.

It's done.

Bella looked down at her plate. She hadn't eaten a mouthful, and the gravy was congealing, the carrots limp. She leaned back in her chair, closed her eyes. She wanted to be a child again: if she couldn't see it, perhaps it wasn't there. But it was – her life – it was relentlessly present, and now Kate was going to be in it again.

Well, that was what Georgie thought.

Bella could still put up a fight.

11

In the night, Bella heard the rain, great sheets of it sluicing her roof and pouring down the gutter. She pictured the bending boughs of the trees, the puddles forming in the street, the sodden earth. Nor did it let up, and when the car pulled up outside in the morning, the sky was dark. Bella stayed in her bed listening to the opening and closing of the car doors and the click of the lock, Georgie's feet slapping wetly as she ran out to meet Kate.

Bella lay there, feeling like a country whose borders had been compromised. There were clangs and clinks coming from the kitchen, Georgie talking loudly and cheerily, Kate's voice low and subdued. She was going to have to go down to see her, or Kate would be brought upstairs. Bella was determined to be the one who controlled the element of surprise, if it was going to be there at all.

When she pushed open the kitchen door, the silence fell immediately. Georgie was at the sink, rinsing out a cup. An old lady sat at the kitchen table, leaning on her elbows, her white hair thin and puffy. Her cheekbones and fine nose gave her a sharp profile.

You're here.

Bella, yes, it's me. Are you pleased to see me?

Bella looked at Georgie, who had stopped mid-action and was watching them both carefully. Bella walked towards Kate, as Kate pushed her hands on the table to stand. Slightly tipping, she leaned towards Bella and put her arms out. Bella took her hands, the knuckles bony, the skin mottled and stretched but the fingers long and elegant, the nails beautifully filed. Kate closed her eyes and Bella leaned in, kissed the hollow in her cheek, then let go.

She could smell the stale face powder.

Bella turned to Georgie, who understood, put down the cup and left the kitchen.

I don't know if I'm pleased to see you, Kate. It's hard to know what I think.

Kate nodded. She sat back down and folded her hands on her lap. She appeared to think for a few moments, then looked back up at Bella, and something of her old fire was back. Bella could see it.

I know I look a shock. I haven't eaten properly for months.

Why not?

Oh, you don't want to know about all that now.

Bella nodded. Kate was right. She didn't want to know.

Why have you come here? Why, after all this time, is it me you would choose?

I have nowhere else to go.

What happened? Where's Alex, and Charlie?

They both died.

Your boy, Charlie? Your sweet boy?

Yes, when he was nineteen. He was never happy but it was an accident. Drugs. Alex died eleven months ago. He told me there was money but there wasn't.

Nothing?

Nothing. I had to sell the house we'd lived in for twenty years but I didn't like it anyway, I didn't mind that. I no longer wanted to be there. Everyone calls those tropical places paradise, but paradise is boring. I wanted to come home to the rain and the wind.

But where?

I didn't know, I could only trust that it would work out somehow. I took a place in the home and paid for six months with the last of what I had. I don't know what I thought, that they would take pity on me—

They did.

Roger did, he is a kind man. But they don't look after you if you have no money.

There are other places. Not everyone can afford to pay for a place in a long-term care facility.

Yes, you're right, there are other places. I saw one or two of them . . .

She didn't need to say any more. Bella had seen them for herself, too, not least when her grandmother was dying. The people were kind, it wasn't that. It was the constant reminder that death lay waiting to seize, and few had the strength to see him off.

But I'm sure I would have found a way – I could still, Bella. I'm not going to force you to keep me—

We'll talk about that but tell me more.

Roger, at the home, he was determined to find somewhere for me to go. I tried to explain to him that I had no more family here – my parents are long dead – and no friends. Alex and I cut everyone off when we left, it seemed the best way.

Why did you leave?

I thought you would have seen it in the papers.

Randall.

Yes.

I saw the headlines.

Kate gave Bella a long look before she went on.

After the inquest and the funeral, Alex wanted to leave. So we went. There was no one we could stand to talk to. Either people would say nothing, as if he had never existed, or they would ask questions we didn't want to answer. Whatever anyone tried to do or say, it was the wrong thing. I didn't blame them. It seemed as if we'd have a better chance under blue skies. But it turned out the old phrase is right, and troubles follow you everywhere. So we stayed when Charlie died.

I'm sorry, I didn't know.

Perhaps I could have told you. I thought about it. But I'd seen a review or two of your exhibitions in the papers, you were obviously fine, happier without me. What would have been the point? We'd parted on such terrible terms, with too many questions left unanswered. It was too soon.

Kate stopped. She was breathing heavily. Bella got up and fetched her a glass of water, passed it across the table.

Thank you.

Kate drank the water, then sat up a little straighter. Put her head to one side. It was coquettish, almost funny in a woman her age, but Bella saw the woman she'd known.

It's good to see you, Bella. You look well.
Better than me.

I don't know about that. You just need a decent feed. You'll get that here, I've become quite a good cook.

Are you saying I can stay?

Not yet, Kate. I'm saying we'll see, for a few days.

That's all I need for now.

12

There was a spare bedroom on the first floor. Georgie, in her efficient way, had already dusted it, put on clean sheets and puffed up the pillows. Kate had two suitcases with her, nothing more. Bella sat on the bed while Kate unpacked.

Is this all your worldly goods?

Yes. I sent a shipping crate over but when it arrived I didn't want any of it. I was never going to read those books again, I had no need for a chair or pictures, and no one who would want them. Roger got rid of it for me, I don't know how, I didn't really care.

He might have sold some things – it could have paid for some more time there.

Perhaps but if he made any money from it, I'm glad. It wouldn't have fetched much.

Kate pulled a long dress out of the suitcase, black silk.

I don't know why I kept this except that I love it. I can't see myself wearing it again.

You never know. There are hangers in the wardrobe you can use.

Thank you.

You always loved your clothes, I felt so scruffy by comparison.

Did you? I don't remember thinking that. But it's true I used to enjoy dressing and I've looked after things so they last. This skirt I've got on must be twenty-five years old.

Kate put down the trousers she had been about to hang and came and sat on the bed beside Bella. Kate's concave chest struggled to breathe.

Is it asthma?

No, no. My heart I think. What was I saying—Oh yes, my old clothes. I made them last but for what? I can't remember why. Can you remember why you did things when you were young?

I don't know, Kate. I look back on myself at that time and it's like watching a film, isn't it? I know I said things and did things but I can't remember the tangible sensations.

Yet, we still feel like we're the same people.

Yes, that's true. It's a shock to look in the mirror.

Oh! Don't talk about that. I avoid that as much as possible. No, I like to remember, it comforts me. I remember us together and I think about my parents. I used to be quite awful to them, I feel badly about that now. Do you remember your mother?

No, I hardly knew her and whatever I did know faded long ago. I think about Granny, how good she was to look after me at a time in her life when she must have been looking forward to putting her feet up a bit. I don't think I was very sympathetic to her, either.

Yes you were.

No, I wasn't. I resented the care she needed and I couldn't understand what the difficulties were for her. I understand now.

None of us understood then. I was a selfish creature in all sorts of ways.

Are you saying that is behind you now?

Kate gave Bella a sideways look and they both laughed.

I'm not promising.

Yes, that's the Kate I know.

What about you, Bella-moo? Why are you alone?

I have Georgie, I'm not completely stranded. But yes, I don't see her as much as I would like. I left David after – well, after all that. It was just Georgie and me for a long time, which was fine. I was painting, and doing quite well.

I know, I told you, I saw the reviews.

Yes, they were mostly kind. That said, I've never painted anything too controversial.

Apart from—

I'm not going to talk about that now, Kate.

No.

I mean it. There is something to be said for you being here but I cannot be dragged back to the past. I don't look back, I never have.

No, my darling. I promise I won't do that. At least, I'll try very hard not to do it. I don't know what it is, Bella, but my mind seems to go backwards without my asking it to. Doesn't yours?

It's not in the habit, I suppose.

You were saying – about you and Georgie.

Yes, we were fine. And she saw David, he was a good father. He married again, and that has kept him happy.

He's still alive?

Oh, yes. David will bury us all.

But then you married again?

I did, Harry. We had fourteen happy years together. I felt lucky to get that chance. We didn't do much – I painted and he pottered, mostly, looking after me. He'd already done his work, sold his business, didn't have anything to prove.

Did he have children?

No, his first wife couldn't have any.

Bella slapped her hands on her thighs.

That's enough of all that. I'm going to talk to Georgie, I know she'll want to push off. We'll have lunch. And then, we'll see.

Yes.

I don't know how I feel about any of this, Kate. It's been sprung on me alarmingly fast, which is typical of Georgie and I should be used to it but I'm not.

Yes.

Then again, we're old women, aren't we? What have we got to lose?

Each other, Bella. And I don't think I could stand it again.

13

There was a routine of sorts, after a month. The mornings were quiet: Kate would have tea in bed, a late bath; Bella got up early to paint. Lunch, and the afternoon was shopping for food or a gentle walk. Kate made the drinks at half-past six, Bella cooked supper. Georgie had gone home, back to her husband and son, her work. She telephoned but Bella preferred that she – and Kate – were left to their own devices. So long as nothing was said out loud, she could pretend she hadn't committed to having Kate back in her life, let alone that they were living together. Neither she nor Kate talked about the future and she wondered if this was part of getting old, relinquishing plans, living completely in the present. And, the past. An oddly new sensation for Bella but in those conversations Kate would be at her most lucid and reflective.

Do you remember how it felt to be married?

It's not so long ago since Alex died. Yes, I remember.

No, in the early days. When you were a young bride. A child bride, you called yourself once.

Goodness, I was. Twenty-one. Barely out of the traps.

Can you remember what it felt like?

I think I felt as if I'd won the prize. Not that Alex was a prize so much as that I had beaten other women in the race to the altar.

Is that why you did it? Get married, that is. I would have imagined you would—

Play the field? I did that quite exhaustively, or so it felt, before I met Alex. He was persuasive, very in love with me, and that's always hard to resist. I knew I wanted to be an actress, I expected to kiss lots of leading men and that they would give me the variety I needed. Alex would always mean safety, home. He didn't let me down in that way.

Was safety what you wanted? I thought you wanted excitement.

Deep down, it must have been. My parents were happily married, even with all the affairs. Do you remember my father telling me that monogamy wasn't a good idea?

Oh my goodness, yes, you were only twelve. That was his idea of the birds and the bees talk.

I know. He explained years later that he and my mother could separate family life from their desire to have sex with other people, and I came to understand that. Alex might have been safe but I was not.

No. Did you have other affairs? Other than . . . I can't remember his name. The man you knew from your childhood summers.

John. That one fizzled out quickly. Yes, I did, until Charlie died. Nothing serious – I never fell in love with anyone. I liked the thrill of the hunt but one where I was the fox, rather than the one riding out to the hounds. Usually, I would escape their clutches at the last second but they would believe they had caught me.

Only you had caught them.

Yes, I was the one with the satisfaction. Or that was how I saw it. What about you? How did you feel about marriage?

When I married David I was so in love with him I was in that mad state. It was why I forgave him anything. So long as he came back to me, I'd overlook it. Marriage didn't give me any feeling of safety when it turned out that he was just as liable to disappear.

Where did he go when he disappeared?

I don't know, but it wasn't drink or drugs. It wasn't even other women. I think when things overwhelmed him he needed to retreat to a cave in some way, to gather his strength and then come back to us.

Those men, they were all-consuming, weren't they?

All those hours we spent devoted to attracting them, keeping them, pleasing them. I don't know that that's even what they wanted.

Oh, I think it is. Men are romantics, they're the ones who remember the scent we wore, who long for a glimpse of our skin. When we're working to please them, they love it.

Perhaps. But then I think they love it when we don't focus everything on them, it gives both sides independence. Harry liked my working, did everything he could to support it.

Yes, because he had already achieved what he wanted.

Or it was because we were no longer young, either of us. Out of the race. We worried less about what anyone else thought and could concentrate on each other.

Is that where we are now?

I certainly don't worry what anyone else thinks.

Nor do I. But also, we can concentrate on each other. No wretched men or children to distract. Have you forgiven me?

For what?

For everything.

I think I tried to forget. There's nothing left to forgive, Kate.

But that's the trouble, one doesn't forget.

I do.

I'd like to believe that.

Then, try.

14

∞

In the dark, they lay together. There was a light on, in the hall, so they could make out the outlines of things as their eyes adjusted. The curtains were drawn, the room was warm. They lay on top of the blankets, another one drawn over them, each wrapped in their dressing gowns. The radio played a piano sonata, softly.

How long is it since we last did this?

A hundred years.

Oh, don't say that. Let's pretend we are young, here in the dark.

All those years between, Kate. What were they for?

We've lived our lives, I suppose.

Yes, but they're nothing but memories now. Stories, mostly forgotten. I feel as if my life is a book on a dusty shelf. Unless I'm opened up, there's no one to read the words.

I'm here. I'll read your words.

Yes. You even wrote some of them with me. Can you remember when we very first knew each other?

We were six. We knew we would be friends straight away.

Did we? Perhaps we did.

I always loved you, Bella.

I don't think I knew that when we were younger, when we were seventeen.

At seventeen, hardly anyone believes it's possible for someone else to love them.

No, and yet you long for it, more than anything. I had that crush on that boy, remember?

Oh, do I! I got into trouble for that one.

Yes, you did. I minded terribly. It seemed like betrayal, at the time. Everything was so much more intense then.

There was more at stake. There was a lot to win, and a lot to lose.

Yes.

I kissed you, Bella. Do you remember?

I do.

I remember wanting to kiss you, very much. It was different to kissing a man.

Yes, much softer, almost shockingly so.

I thought: this is what men feel. It's so different to what women feel.

Scratchy chins and firm muscles.

Oh, I miss that, too.

Yes, so do I.

But I didn't just mean how it felt like that, I meant my reasons for wanting to kiss you were different.

Bella wriggled a little, in the dark. She heard someone walking in the street outside. It was late to them, her and Kate, but not to the rest of the world. The world never seemed to sleep any more.

What were your reasons?

With men, I wanted to convince them of my beauty. It was a show, each time. But with you, I wanted to possess you, to hold you and to comfort you.

I can't remember what I felt about it. I think I felt confused.

Yes, that's understandable.

We dreamt once of leaving the men, and just living together in a house of our own with the children.

We should have done it. Life would have been much simpler.

I don't know if that's true. I don't think the two of us are necessarily uncomplicated with each other. I don't think we would have been back then, either. All the things one minded about, and raising children is hard. We forget that now.

Yes, I know I got it wrong.

Oh, Kate, I'm so sorry. I didn't mean it like that. You didn't do wrong by Charlie.

But I did. People try to tell me that he was an unhappy person and it wouldn't have mattered what any of us had said or done, but I don't believe that's true. You can't, or you'd never try to help anyone.

No, one must always try to help. And listen. But when children grow up and leave, we can't control all the forces to which they are vulnerable. And you did your best.

That's just it, Bella. I don't think I did. I was selfish. I cared more about what I was doing, what I wanted. I loved Charlie, very much, but I didn't think he needed me. He was a boy. I thought that meant he had everything easily, that there was no need to fight.

Some people are born insecure.

Some have insecurity thrust upon them.

Tell me the good things about Charlie. I'd like to know.

Yes, it's better to remember him as he was. He was shy, which exasperated me, of course, but Alex was sympathetic. He was clever, I think. He became obsessed with the solar system, would lie for hours in his room, looking through the telescope at the stars beyond his window. In the dark.

Like we are now.

Yes. Darling Charlie.

Kate cried and Bella reached out for her hand. They gripped each other tightly, their palms dry. Then she stopped, and loosened her hold.

Did you always blame me for that terrible accident with Georgie?

The jam. Yes, I did, for a very long time. I thought there would be scars, but there weren't. What stayed longer was the shock of what might have been.

You see, I knew you hadn't forgotten everything you needed to forgive me for.

In a way I had. It's more that I let go of it when I finally recognised that Georgie was growing up happy. If she is messed up in any way – and who isn't? – that's down to me and David, not that accident.

The shock of what might have been. I think that was why I behaved so badly afterwards. The guilt made me defensive, made me go on the attack.

Perhaps that's it.

And I'm sorry I didn't listen to you about Randall.

That's all right.

No, it's not. I felt guilt for that too, you see.

It was nothing to do with you.

He was my stepson.

Yes, but that didn't make him do what he did.

I shouldn't have dismissed it, when you told me.

We did, in those days. We thought that was what men did to women. It was something to put up with. Quite a lot of the time, we told ourselves we didn't even mind it.

Yes, we did do that. But it was wrong. I told him, Bella, what he'd done. When Alex was there, that night, just before he—

Shush. Let's not talk about that.

No.

Upsetting things should be put away.

Yes, they're all gone. Now it's just us.

Yes, Katie. Now it's just us.

15

Shall I go to the shops for you, Bella?

No thank you, we don't need anything.

Butter? Milk? Some bread?

No, I think we're fine for all of those things. If you look in the fridge, Kate, you'll see we've got about four pints in there.

I'd like to go to the shops for you, I'd like to be useful.

I know, and I love your help, but you have been to the shops twice today already.

Have I?

Yes, you have.

Perhaps I could go just to pick up a little treat for us. Some nice chocolate. You'd like that, wouldn't you?

You've done that too, Katie. I can't eat any more chocolate, and nor should you. Your teeth—

I'm not going to the dentist.

No, if you're not in any pain, but when I go for my check-up—

No.

Katie, don't worry, I'm not going to make you go.

Bella, do you remember when we used to play princesses?

Did we?

Oh, yes, we did. We would go on a search for handsome princes.

That sounds fun.

I think it was. I think we used to dress up. Yes, we were naughty little things, we would go into my mother's wardrobe and take out her dresses.

Did she mind?

I think she did. You broke a necklace of hers.

Goodness, she can't have been pleased about that.

No, but I was. I could keep it because it was broken. I wonder where it is. Perhaps it's upstairs in my box?

Maybe. Do you want to go up and look in your box? There's lots of things in there you like to look at.

No, I think I'll go to the shops. Do you need anything, Bella? I'd like to be helpful. What can I get you, from the shops? Maybe a nice treat for us both, that would be good.

16

In the kitchen, the radio was on. Two men, talking. Bella washed the leeks, then cut them. She was bent over the work-top, holding her knife carefully. Her grip was less certain now and the blade might slip, too easily, and she was frightened of a flow of blood. Cuts were no longer easily staunched by plasters and took weeks to heal. When she had finished, she used the same knife to sweep the leeks into a steamer. Only then did she happen to glance at the kitchen table behind her, where Kate was sitting with her drink, more tonic than gin, and lots of ice.

Kate's head was in her hands and she was muttering softly: no, no.

Bella said her name, and Kate looked up with eyes that had gone as pale as a puddle, full of fear.

I don't understand what they are talking about. Please, make them go away. Shut it up, *shut it up*, Bella.

SEVENTY-NINE

1

∞

Kate, don't you think you ought to get dressed today?

Why?

You haven't got out of your nightdress for
three days now.

There's nothing unusual about that. I never
get dressed.

Yes, you do. I'm going to go down and make lunch and
it will be ready in half an hour. Be dressed for lunch,
won't you?

No. I'm not doing what you tell me to do. You're not
my mother.

I'm not telling you, I'm asking.

I don't see why I should. I'm perfectly comfortable like
this. I wish you would stop telling me what to do. I
wish you would go away.

I'm not going anywhere. This is my house.

Your house, is it? Are you telling me to leave? Sorry, *asking* me to leave?

No—

Fine. I'll go. I'll make you really happy, I'll go outside and pour petrol over myself and set fire to myself. Shall I do that?

Yes, why don't you do that while I go and make lunch?

2

Mum, we're worried that it's too much for you, too much work.

No, it's not. I'm perfectly fine. The doctor said I have the heart of a woman half my age.

Yes, but Kate is—

I know what she is, and it will pass.

Mum, it's going to get worse, not better. It's only got worse for the last two years.

That's relative. She's not angry any more. I don't know what that was but it's over now and I promise you there is nothing I can't cope with. It will get better.

How can you say that?

Because we're old and getting older.

Exactly. I've looked into some options and—

I'm not looking at any options. Will you let me make my own decisions?

Yes.

I know you're only looking after me.

Yes, Mum, that is what I'm doing.

But I'm perfectly capable.

How is she today?

She's fine. She's eating a little more, lately. We talk. We have a lot to talk about, even after all this time.

When she's lucid.

She is lucid.

It's as if you're having a conversation with a different person. She repeats herself.

In a way we are talking to two different people, Georgie. She's not nervous around me, and we talk about the past. She knows you all think she's going mad.

I don't think that. It's just—

Leave it, darling.

All right, for the moment. Are you painting?

Yes, I keep busy, if that's what you're asking.

I know you do. You'll ask for help, if you need it, won't you?

Yes, my darling, I promise. I will. But I won't need it.
We're tough old birds, we'll see this through.

That's true, I expect. It's a good thing you've
done, you know.

What?

Having Kate to live with you. Not giving up on her.

That's not the way I see it. We're in it together,
whatever it is. I'm not alone now, Georgie, and
nor is Kate.

So that's good.

It is, my darling. It is.

3

Bella, I want to go home.

This is your home, Kate. Remember? You live here, with me.

No, I want to go home, to my house.

You sold your house. Look, here are your things: your glasses, your book. Your coat is hanging in the hall. We can go for a walk soon.

Where is Alex? Why can't he come and get me?

Alex isn't here. He hasn't been with you for a long time.

No. You're right, I can't find him. I looked for him this morning and he wasn't here. Is he at work?

Perhaps he is. Would you like to go for a walk?

I don't know, I don't know what I want to do. Won't you tell me?

Here, Katie, wipe those tears away. Today is not a good day but tomorrow will be better. We'll step outside, nice and cosy in our warm coats, and we'll look at the birds, and the people. Then we can come back and sit together. I will paint, and you can listen to the radio.

Don't leave me, Bella.

I won't, I'm right here. Hold my hand, see? I'm not going anywhere.

EIGHTY-TWO

1

❤

Each Sunday afternoon, sitting in the kitchen, a ritual: the counting of the pills. Into the little boxes, one for each day. Pink in the morning, blue at lunch, yellow before bed. They measure out the week in dawn's colours. Over time, Bella had gathered a separate stash of the yellow ones, in case. Not too many, just enough.

2

Kate's favourite chair was the one by the window, overlooking the little patch of garden in front and the street outside. She would watch people walk past. The mothers in the morning, pushing the prams with babies, older children trotting beside them, schoolbags bouncing on their backs. The postman on his rounds who gave a cheery wave on sunny days, a grimace when it was raining. A smartly dressed man with a neat moustache on his way to the office, they presumed, though he went at funny hours; Kate and Bella – admittedly, mostly Bella – would speculate on the possible nature of his work. The favoured option was spy, though they conceded it was more likely to be a vague title they didn't understand, like 'consultant'.

By Kate's side, a low table, piled with half-finished activities: crossword books; letters; knitting. Some of her old theatre programmes were there and Kate would recount to Bella the personalities of the other actors, the mishaps that had occurred on the stage. That time she had completely dried and the cue had to whisper every word of her lines for the rest of the performance.

Three times a day, a cup of tea, with a biscuit. A nice woman called Janet came around daily, except the weekends, to bring the shopping and help Bella with lunch. She would change the bedsheets, wash Kate's often soaked clothes, accidents that were too regular to be called as such. Once a month Janet and Bella would batch cook suppers for the freezer. Bella was still painting, even with no exhibition in sight. It gave her a freedom she found exhilarating, to try new things, and return to the old, reawakening the dormant. She had started doing portraits again.

Georgie came more often, sometimes with her boy. Kate called him Charlie, and he didn't stop her, said he could see it pleased her, let's leave it.

The days were long, and quiet. There was enough to be getting on with. It was just as they liked it. In the evenings, after supper was cleared away, Bella would read and Kate would listen, her eyes closed. Sometimes, Bella would stop and read to herself but Kate did not protest.

3

∞

Bella. *Bella.*

Yes?

I'm so sorry I kissed that boy.

What boy?

The boy you liked . . . I'm so sorry. I can't
remember his name.

Oh, Katie. There's nothing to be sorry for.

Yes, there is, there *is.* You liked him, and I knew it.

It's too long ago. Don't upset yourself.

I was such a wicked child.

Oh, well. You were certainly naughty. I don't think
you were wicked.

Everyone said I was. They said so, when
Mr Garfield—

What?

He was our teacher, do you remember?

I do. What about him?

Everyone said it was my fault. But it wasn't. That one
time. It wasn't. But all the other times, I have been
bad, Bella. An awful person. I hurt the people who
loved me most.

Kate, at her smallest now, an old woman, with skin like tracing
paper and eyes like a winter's dawn, shrank even further into
herself. Her voice tremulous, belonging to a frightened child.

I think we all do that, at some time or other, Kate. But,
please. Don't upset yourself now. Mr Garfield will
have been dead a long time. Forget about it.

Kate shook her head, as if trying to throw something off.

No, no, no. I have to, I have to say it. I should have said
it long ago, how sorry I am. I wish I could say sorry to
Alex for John.

Did he ever know?

I don't know. Alex was such a sweet man.

I know.

He was good to me and I was never good to him.

That's not true. You were married a long time.

Oh. Yes, we were, weren't we?

Yes.

Do you still love me, Bella-moo?

Yes, I do. You know I do.

And everything will be all right, won't it?

Yes, of course it will. Come on now, we should have some supper. Are you hungry?

No. I don't want much. Some bread and jam.

If you like.

Yes, please. Yes I would. Some bread and jam. It wasn't me, you know that, don't you?

Wasn't you what?

Randall, when he—

Randall?

Yes. I did believe you, you know, I knew what he had done but I couldn't say anything. Not then.

No.

Then I did.

You said something?

Yes, I told Alex and Randall was there. We were all there, looking at your painting. You left the gun in there, didn't you Bella?

304

Yes.

But how did you find the key?

Georgie told me, she saw it, in the matchbox on your dressing table.

The matchbox. Covered in seed pearls.

Yes.

Why did you put the gun in there?

I don't know. A symbol of my anger, perhaps.

Did you mean for it to happen?

What?

Randall. He—

I don't know, Kate. I'm so sorry. But I think I must have. I wanted something to happen. I wanted him punished. And you.

I think you did. And we were punished.

Yes.

The safety catch was off, Bella. That's what Alex said, afterwards. Was that you?

Yes.

Oh, Bella.

How did it happen?

I don't know. That is, I do but I don't want to. I don't think about it.

Take it slowly, but tell me.

Randall went to get it, and I tried to take it off him, and Alex was there, too, and then—

Go on.

I don't know, Bella. I don't know what happened.

Yes, yes, you do, Kate. You have to tell me.

When did it happen, Bella?

A long time ago.

Will the police come? I'm afraid to tell. Alex said—

They won't come now. No one needs to know. But I want to. Please, tell me, Kate.

I shot him, Bella. I shot him, for you.

For me?

The gun went off, it was so loud and there was so much blood.

I'm so sorry, Kate.

All that blood, and Alex was screaming. I think I was too, I can't remember much.

Tell me what you can, what do you see, in your mind's eye?

I can't see anything, not of the moment it happened. Only after and I was crying and Alex said not to say anything about who was holding the gun because Randall was dead and Alex said, he said—

What did he say?

He said the blood was on all our hands, Bella. And it was, you know. It's still there.

That's why you left the country?

Yes.

I'm so sorry, Kate.

No, Bella, it is me who is sorry, so sorry. Bella, can you take me to bed now please? I'm very tired.

Yes, Kate. We'll go to bed now, we'll sleep.

I'm so tired. I only want to sleep.

You will, I promise.

4

∞

On that night, they went up the stairs, brushed their teeth and washed their faces. Kate sang a snatch of a schoolgirl rhyme; it made Bella laugh. Then Bella gave Kate the yellow pills, measured out and eased down with gulps of hot milk. They got into bed together, Kate's back warm, curled against Bella's chest, their legs drawn up, their hands held. The light was put out and in the dark they stayed afloat. Outside, the branches of the tree bent a little in the wind, and the rain did not come.

Acknowledgements

THANK YOU

To my editors, Ed Wood and Catherine Richards, who gave me the tools to find my voice and the courage to use it.

To Rebecca Wearmouth, who instigated this book and encouraged me to write it against lockdown odds.

To Eugenie Furniss, agent extraordinaire.

To Ellen Rockwell, for the beautiful cover design.

To my grandmother, Kate, who gave me ideas.

To my mother, Georgina, and her best friend, Clare, who taught me how good friendship can be.

To my best friends, who are decidedly not in this book and make the good parts of real life even better: Celia, Anna, Mary, Emma, Emily, Flo, Mhairi, Lydia, Alexa, Claire, Sharon, Luisa and Kate.

To my family, Simon, Beatrix, Louis and George, who are everything.

More Reading from Jessica Fellowes

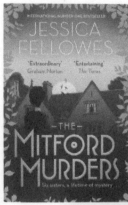

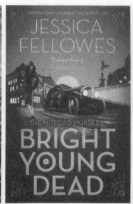

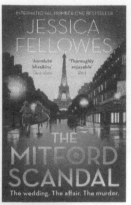

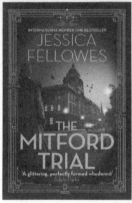

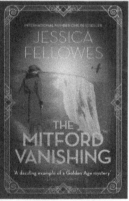